HOLLOW BRIDGE PUBL

UNTHINKABLE SINS 2:
THE FAMILY
A NOVEL

TIFFANI QUARLES-SANDERS

Unthinkable Sins 2: The Family
Copyright © 2016 by Tiffani Quarles-Sanders

⁎ PROLOGUE ⁐

"Everything bad I ever done was because of the love caught up in it. What have you ever done for love?"

Hattie Durham,
Unthinkable Sins

"**W**hat?!" The staffers in the busy lobby of Jerome Durham's campaign headquarters heard the agitated shout from the inner office and immediately became alert. Councilman Durham's opponent in that year's mayoral campaign was being interviewed, and they were tuned to the TV in the storefront reception area. Up until now, Ted Lawson hadn't said much of anything interesting, and some of the workers had stopped watching the broadcast. But the white-haired Lawson had just insulted his opponent, calling Jerome Durham's agenda on crime "passive" and "ineffective." The staff knew that his wife, Susan, had heard the same comments on the television in her office. If Jerome Durham had been at the office that day, no one would have been concerned. But now everyone tried to appear busy knowing his wife was on the war path.

"The councilman's policies would result in higher crime rates across the city and all because the man is afraid to offend one community by taking tougher measures in areas where they're really needed," Lawson said. "This city would only suffer under Mr. Durham, who is inexperienced in the level of stewardship needed to guide a municipality of this size." Lawson looked at the camera with a smile. "If you're watching, Councilman

Durham, you're a good-looking man, I'll admit. But as city leader, you are – simply – weak."

"Weak!" Susan's scream rang through the office. She appeared in the doorway, petite and furious, in a dove grey designer suit. "Are we recording this? Somebody please tell me we are recording this."

An attractive girl of about 17 looked up from her computer screen. "Yes, we are, Auntie. I set the timer on the DVR out here and on the VCR in your office, just like you asked. But even if we didn't get it, we could probably just find it on the Internet later."

It was exactly the wrong thing to say to Susan when she had just heard her husband slandered on TV by that white-haired buffoon Larson. She glared at her niece.

"I've asked you to address me as 'Aunt Susan' when we're in the office, Lashonna, and we won't be waiting around to do anything later. If we are to stay on top of this campaign, we always have to be prepared to do whatever it takes right now!"

There was silence as the staff looked around at each other. Deflated, Lashonna slunk down in her chair. Across the room, her twin Latasha frowned and stood up from leaning against the copy machine. She was notoriously protective of her sister. Their mother, Donetta, who was also volunteering that day, walked over and put her hand on Lashonna's shoulder. She threw Latasha a warning glance, but Susan had already pinned the girl with a challenging stare of her own, quickly silencing any sharp words Latasha may have pitched her aunt's way. Both Latasha and Lashonna needed these volunteer internships as well as good references from her for their college applications, so Susan wasn't going to tolerate any mess from these girls.

Donetta was relieved to see Latasha back down and close her mouth. Latasha rolled her eyes and tried to catch Lashonna's eye so that they could plan to get together later to talk about how mean their aunt was. The reason they were all doing this was for Jerome, anyway, not his bossy wife. In the meantime, Susan had moved on.

"Well, come on, Team Durham. Who can think of some things we can do right now to make sure Lawson does not get the last word here?" Susan ranted. "We will not just sit and take it quietly while Ted Lawson says things like that about my husband on national TV."

"Councilman Durham would say to take the high road and just ignore it," said an earnest volunteer named Bobby Gray. "He doesn't like making negative comments."

"Exactly right. And since we can't fight fire with fire, we need another response. We can't afford to just ignore it," Susan said. She began to pace up and down the room. "What I want us to do is make sure Lawson's negative comments get drowned out in a flood of positive things being said about our candidate. How can we do that?" said Susan, trying to rally the office into action. When no one responded, she prompted them. "What's the best way to generate that flood and get people saying great things about Jerome?"

Susan continued to pace as she brainstormed furiously and the staff whispered amongst themselves. "All right, first of all, he needs to be seen in as many places as possible doing good things," she said. "And we need to beef up his social calendar. I want a list of people we can call, and to schedule some appropriate dinners and outings and things like that. Harry, can you get me that?"

Harry nodded and quickly scurried away.

Susan paused, her forehead creasing in thought, before rapidly calling out her next series of orders. "We need to scour the town for any events or happenings of any kind that might be going on in the next few days to which we haven't already been invited and arrange to get invited. Or arrange to be close to places where anything at all is happening, and make sure the media is there. Donetta, can you handle that?"

Donetta stood near Lashonna with her hand on her shoulder. She didn't like the way Susan had spoken to her daughter and wanted to comfort the girl. "Yes, Susan. I got Jerome's current schedule ... I mean, Councilman Durham's schedule ... right here," Donetta said.

Susan winced at Donetta's grammar. Donetta sank into the chair next to Lashonna and looked at the calendar on her screen. Susan walked over and looked over her shoulder.

"Team, I'm serious, we have to scour for every likely opportunity," said Susan, scanning the computer screen and making note of a gap in that afternoon's event calendar. She issued a last general command to the staff members, who were already moving rapidly. "Somebody get my husband on the phone, and let me talk to him. We don't have anything scheduled this evening until after 6 p.m., so see what you can find before that. I can have him ready by 2," she said.

Buzzing with importance, Susan stepped away from

Donetta and took the phone from the girl who had dialed the councilman at home. "Honey, did you see Lawson's interview?" Her sugar-sweet voice had a hard-coated edge to it.

"Yes, honey, I saw." Jerome held the phone away from his ear as the headache he was nursing made everything seem extra loud. He had stayed home from the office, planning to let the aspirin do its job while he worked in quiet. But Susan had other ideas. Instead of shaking off his competitor's offhand comments, she wanted to launch a full-on assault of publicity spotlighting his good deeds and virtues.

After a few minutes of useless protests, Jerome wearily agreed to her plan. Susan usually knew best, anyway. At least he could have the next couple of hours in peace; knowing his wife, she would be issuing a final round of orders down at the campaign office before hurrying to get her hair and nails done. Susan would never dream of being caught before a camera without a fresh, professional polishing-up, and it sounded like she would be sharply on the lookout for lenses this day. Jerome didn't think Lawson's comments were that big a deal, but they had gotten Susan fired up. He trusted her instincts, and there was no harm in being motivated to step things up.

As weary as he was, Jerome took a moment to be thankful for Susan. As always, she was incredibly quick-minded and business savvy, at times seeming more dedicated to his success than he was himself. Susan would never let a little thing like feeling tired keep her from making every effort to see that people saw him in the most flattering light. She seemed tireless, and Jerome marveled at her energy.

Determined to be worthy of his wife's efforts, Jerome washed a handful of vitamins down with a glass of orange juice and headed for the shower. He stood under the warm spray, willing it to revive him, as he thought about whom he would talk to and what he would say at the last-minute appearances Susan had booked for the afternoon. He had been feeling tired and having headaches more often lately.

Jerome thought maybe he would squeeze in a visit to the doctor for some vitamin shots; that ought to put the pep back in his step and help him get through what was proving to be a grueling campaign. He told himself he still wanted the mayor's office more than anything. In that role, he could do more to help the community in bigger and better ways than ever before. With Susan at his side, he could still reach for it. But could he hold on to it? With the way he had been feeling lately, Jerome wasn't entirely sure. He shook the thought off and headed for the wardrobe to find what he hoped was the perfect tie for whatever last-minute appearance his woman had in mind.

Back at the office, Susan had outwardly calmed down a bit, but, internally, she was just getting started. She ordered her niece Latasha to work the DVR for her as she watched the Lawson interview over and over, seething over his damaging words. It irked her that there was no chance for a direct rebuttal, as Jerome had already appeared on the same show yesterday. Her husband had refused to be baited by the interviewer into saying things against his opponent. When the interview was offered to him, Jerome had thought it good fortune that he'd been asked to appear first, thinking that he could set the agenda by promoting policies he thought would be good for the community. Now, Susan thought, maybe that had not been such a good idea.

As if she had read her sister-in-law's mind, Donetta said, "Susan, just so you know, I'm also reviewing any other broadcast interviews the councilman has set up to make sure that he's always scheduled last when they're going to be talking to both candidates."

Susan stopped and looked thoughtfully at Donetta for a moment. Her comment showed a remarkably astute grasp of the situation, something Susan wouldn't have thought Donetta capable of having. Initially, Susan hadn't been too sure about asking her sister-in-law to help out with Jerome's campaign, however, they simply could not afford to turn down all the help they could get. But the cheerful younger woman was actually turning out to be quite useful after all. She was great at keeping her twin daughters and the other volunteers in line. Donetta could also both type- and talk-up a storm at the same time, and she didn't seem to mind running errands all over town, as long as she could use her sister-in-law's big, black Mercedes sedan.

"Donetta, if you'd like to come back tomorrow and the rest of the week, we could use your help," Susan said. She wouldn't yet go as far as to tell her sister-in-law that she'd done a good job, a great job, in fact, and that having her around would be an asset to the campaign.

"Really? I'd love to," Donetta dimpled in pleasure.

She had only planned on working there a few days to supervise the twins and help get things going, but now Susan offered an opportunity she could not turn down. Working in her brother-in-law's campaign office was so much more fun and exciting than sitting around at home all day: there was always something going on, and it was bright and colorful with balloons and banners, and people bustling around all the time. Everybody got especially energized when Jerome was there, too. The councilman laughed and joked with them and made the hard work feel like a party. No doubt, Jerome was far more pleasant and easygoing than his wife.

"I'd wear something else tomorrow, though," Susan said. She eyed her sister-in-law's clothing, barely masking her distaste. "A different hairstyle, perhaps. Maybe something in just one color?"

Donetta nodded. Susan was making an effort to be tactful, but Donetta would not have been offended. It was no secret that Lewis Durham's wife was partial to brightly-colored wigs and wore them just about every day. Today, Donetta's own hair was done up in cornrows beneath the corkscrew-sprigged blonde and copper wig she wore over it. The look suited her, making her appear every bit the live wire she was known to be.

"All right, thank you, Susan," she replied. Her tone was matter-of-fact. "What else?"

"Overall, I think you probably just want to tone it down and dress more conservatively," Susan said. Being invited to do so, Susan did not hesitate now to offer her full opinion. She looked over Donetta's clothing and refrained from shaking her head. "A campaign office is a professional place. Stick to solid colors. A button-down blouse is always a good choice," Susan added, throwing the other woman a bone. The short sleeved shirt Donetta wore today appeared to be polyester with a tie-dye pattern. "Stick to solid colors, and you'll be fine."

Susan realized she was talking as if Donetta was coming on for a long-term position, and, on further consideration, thought that actually would not be a bad idea. She would think it over, and then run her decision by her husband. When he took the mayor's office – as she had no doubt that he would – Donetta's talents might be useful in some capacity. Jerome liked his brother's wife and would go along easily with the idea. It would please him to have more members of his family close at this pinnacle in his career.

Susan tried to picture her sister-in-law in something conservative like the navy suits she herself favored, and the thought made her want to laugh. She doubted the woman owned anything in navy or any other neutral shade, for that matter. In the meantime, Donetta nodded eagerly at Susan's suggestions, grateful for the advice. Susan Chalfont Durham was the best-dressed woman Donetta had ever known, and she felt honored to be getting wardrobe tips from her. With someone like Susan helping her, there was no telling how well she could do.

"Tone it down, be more conservative," Donetta repeated to herself. She wanted to be sure to get it right.

"All right, then. Get me the information for that dealership opening, and see what we can do to get some press there," said Susan, turning her focus back to the campaign. "Maybe there already will be. Councilman

Durham will be congratulating the owner, and talking about how important new businesses like this are when it comes to creating jobs and reducing crime in the community."

Susan smiled, pleased with her ability to spin this last-minute appearance into a chance for Jerome to respond to Lawson's comments. The next thing to do was to have Latasha call the beauty shop, and tell them she wanted to come in for a fresh top coat and hairdo. She didn't worry about them accommodating her; she was the wife of Jerome Durham. Susan went over the rest of the afternoon in her head. She could pick up fresh clothing from the dry cleaners for both her and Jerome on the way home, and they would show up at that dealership looking every inch the power couple that they were.

"My husband is not weak," she whispered to herself. "He's the strongest man I know."

CHAPTER 2

Tall and good-looking, Jerome Durham greeted Susan at the door when she got home later that day, catching her by the waist for a brief hug as she bustled in with their clothing. She patted him on the cheek, then stood back and looked at him.

"Jerome, honey, how are you feeling? Headache all gone?"

Jerome gave her his relaxed smile and nodded. "Yes, ma'am. Good as new."

Susan thought he looked more tired than a man who had spent the morning resting should look, but she didn't have time to worry about that now. She handed him his suit.

"Here," she said. "We have just enough time to get dressed and maybe have a cup of coffee before we go to the opening. You look like you could use it."

Though her comment stung, Jerome laughed it off. He knew she didn't mean anything by it. He knew she just wanted him to look his best and wouldn't have said anything if some improvement wasn't needed. Susan caught his look and gave him a reassuring kiss.

"You are a gorgeous man, Councilman Durham, and this afternoon, at that dealership, in that suit," she winked at him, "you are going to be entirely devastating. You'll have to beat all the lady car buyers off with a stick."

They laughed together and headed upstairs to change.

As he tied his tie before the mirror, Jerome watched Susan walking around in her slip, then stepping into the skirt of a pale peach colored suit. She had always been an attractive woman and still was at 61. Her alabaster skin contained its share of fine lines, but Jerome saw his wife's aging as a refining process rather than a destructive one. He still found her incredibly beautiful.

"Jerome, are you seriously over there daydreaming?"

Jerome was jolted out of his private thoughts. "No, honey. I was just thinking over my remarks for this afternoon."

Susan nodded and paused before the heavy bureau they shared: one side was his and the other was hers. She picked up a framed picture and looked at it. Jerome saw her and spoke before she did.

"I brought that up when I was going over my keynote for tonight," he explained. "It helps when I speak to her picture like she was my audience," he added wistfully. "You know how much Ma'Dear loved to help me get ready for debates, recitals, anything at all when I had an appearance to make."

Susan met his gaze in the mirror, tipping her head in acknowledgement, then put the picture back down. He knew the rules. "Just don't forget to take it back downstairs," she said.

He nodded agreeably and watched her disappear into the bathroom for a second, then reappear in the doorway. Susan knew Jerome missed his mother, Hattie, so she usually indulged him with his memories. But she drew the line at having the woman's picture in their bedroom.

Susan walked back over to her husband and redid his tie.

"This is the perfect tie for the occasion," she said, appreciatively. "Good choice."

Jerome put his hands around Susan's waist and kissed her. "Thank you, Madame," he said grandly.

He held onto her for a moment, but more to steady himself than out of gratitude as a wave of pain and weakness washed over him. He didn't want to alarm Susan, so he kissed her again, then walked over to sit down on the foot of the bed.

"I sure hope you weren't planning on staying at this thing too long," he said. "A dealership opening, for goodness sake!"

"Honey, I know it's not the kind of thing that we have been doing, but you know it's a smart idea for you to appear at more events like this," she said. "It's a way to get out and meet people in the greater community that aren't that familiar with who we are."

"I have no objection to going to this type of event, but scheduling this on top of another event this evening at the last minute is a concern," said Jerome, approaching the topic slowly with the diplomacy of a practiced councilman. "I feel like I should conserve my energy if I'm going to be on top of my game at any of these appearances."

Susan turned to look at him, raising an eyebrow.

"Are you telling me you don't think you're up to it?"

Jerome sighed. "No, that's not what I'm saying," he said, carefully choosing his next words. "It's just that this afternoon is going to be intense, and I stayed home with a headache today. I admit, it will be an effort."

"Well, it's one effort you'll have to make," said Susan, giving her husband a pointed look that brooked no argument. "If you want to win this race, we have to be able to adapt to last-minute scheduling changes and seeing more people. A mayor's race is different than running for city council, as we've discussed, Jerome."

"Yes, my love," said Jerome, conceding. He sighed. "Well, seeing you tonight in your new evening gown will have to be my consolation prize," he said. He stood behind his wife and drew her close.

"That's the spirit," Susan said. She loved it when her husband complimented her, and she looked forward to his reaction to seeing her in her lavender gown tonight. Susan patted Jerome's cheek and checked her hair in the mirror. "That's our next mayor talking."

The couple looked at their reflection in the full-length mirror, looking polished and exuding power. They smiled. Behind them, from a picture frame on the dresser, Mother Hattie Durham smiled too.

D onetta came out wearing a red pantsuit when Susan stopped to pick her and the girls up the next day. Though it wasn't the latest style and the fit was a little snug, Susan thought her sister-in-law's outfit was a lot better than what she'd worn the previous day.

Donetta sported a short, neatly-clipped hairdo in a dark burgundy shade that just missed clashing with her red suit. The wig, if eye-catching, was at least discreet, and not multicolored or too bright in tone.

Typical teenagers, Latasha and Lashonna had either forgiven or – more likely – forgotten the tensions of the previous day. They greeted Susan affectionately as they got into the back seat and even leaned forward to kiss her on the cheek before putting on their seatbelts.

"Good morning, Donetta. You look very nice today," Susan said.

"Thank you so much, Susan. I worked hard to put this together." Donetta glowed from the rare compliment from her sister-in-law. "Did you all have a good time last night? How is my brother-in-law, anyway?"

"Is Uncle Jerome coming to the office today?" Latasha broke in. "I sure hope so."

"Me too," Lashonna added. "He hasn't seen the new posters yet."

"Or mom," Latasha said. "He might not even recognize you, mother."

"And just what do you mean by that?" Donetta laughed good-naturedly. The girls exchanged glances.

"You have to admit that you look ... really different, mommy," said Lashonna, trying to be diplomatic.

Susan was amused. The girls had taken over the conversation, sparing her from having to make small talk when she wanted to concentrate on other things. She couldn't help wondering, though, what Jerome would think about his sister-in-law's transformation. She could hear him now, showering Donetta with compliments. Jerome was the type of man who liked to make people feel good. As for herself, Susan wasn't sure if she liked Donetta's new look or not. She had to admit, the girl cleaned up nicely.

Once they made it to the office, everyone made a fuss over Donetta, causing her already wide smile to grow even wider.

Susan found herself growing annoyed. Donetta was getting far too much attention with her saucy new clothes and hairdo. Today, Susan wore her own hair in a conservative bun at the base of her neck, preventing her from tossing it the way she normally would have done in such a situation. People usually looked her way when she did that. Instead, she sauntered over to the table, exaggerating her movements so that her skirt swished around her legs. She knew some of the men were watching. Some of the women were eyeing her too, with obvious disapproval, but she paid them no mind. Showing a little leg was one of the only respectable ways of attracting male attention left to women of her age. Susan had taken ballet classes as a teenager and still did the strengthening exercises that kept her legs toned and supple. She clapped her hands loudly.

"Councilman Durham will be in some time this morning," she announced. "I'm not sure exactly when, but I think it would be a good idea to show him some progress being made when he does get here. Let's get that mailing out, people. "

This time there was no doubt that everyone was watching as she strode back to the office. Susan could practically feel the daggers in her back. Her announcement had been unnecessary, as everyone felt that Susan had slave-driven them in Jerome's absence. Ironically, they sometimes got less done when he was around, as Jerome was notorious for drawing people into conversations or creating other distractions for them. They all loved the candidate and didn't mind working extra hard for him.

In the office, Susan wondered where Jerome was. He said he had a stop to make before coming in, but he hadn't told her what it was. She was concerned about Jerome after last evening. He had been his usual charming and magnetic self, and, as she'd expected, the women had flocked to him after he gave his address. Susan had to cut in on several of his dances with female admirers, reminding him how important it was for him to circulate. But now she suspected that he was deliberately stretching those dances out, using them as opportunities to rest. Then, they had come home, and he had immediately gone to bed.

She knew just when Jerome got there by the noise

in the outer office. She looked through the window and saw him standing there with several boxes of donuts in his arms. Everyone was gathering around him, of course all wanting a pastry, but they would have done the same thing if he had showed up without any food. Everybody adored Jerome. There was no doubt in her mind whatsoever that he would win the mayor's race.

She waited with impatience for him to finally come to the office. She wondered if he was deliberately personally conversing with everyone out there in order to avoid confronting her. After making such a fuss over seeing her in her evening gown for his keynote speech last night, she was still annoyed by the fact that he had not wanted to make love when they got home. He had not even tried.

Susan knew she had looked good in her evening dress, a slim column of lavender lace. The high neck and sleeves were age appropriate and conservative, the gown itself flattered her still slim figure. Lavender was Jerome's favorite color. Plus, the evening had been successful, and that always got them both worked up. Susan had expected Jerome to seize her the moment they walked through the front door, especially after his comments that afternoon, but he kissed her and headed straight to bed.

Susan had climbed into bed beside Jerome, and, after waiting in the still darkness for him to make a move, she reached for him. Jerome pushed her back gently. "Susan, I'm really wiped out," he said. "See you in the morning." And he had gone promptly to sleep.

Pondering this, Susan stood up to look for Jerome one more time and ran into him just outside the door.

"Good morning, my beautiful wife," he said, kissing her.

"Well, good morning, candidate Durham," she said.

The first thing she noticed was that Jerome looked considerably better this morning. His amber eyes were sparkling, and his skin looked good. He had always been a good looking man: tall, with broad shoulders and a broad, dimpled chin. Jerome Durham was even more of a heartthrob than he had been as a teenager.

Seeing the way the other women at the banquet were drawn to her husband had fanned Susan's desire for him that much more last night. In the past, Jerome had said he felt the same way when he saw other men reacting to her, and last night Susan had received her share of admiring looks. She had gone home feeling desirable and confident, and she wanted to show her man a good time. But he hadn't touched her.

"Where were you this morning? Surely it didn't take two hours to get donuts," she said, closing the door behind him. She heard the sharpness in her tone. She hadn't meant to jump on him right away. But Jerome sat down on the corner of the desk, still smiling.

"No. I stopped by the doctor's office. I wanted to get some vitamin shots," he explained.

"Oh," said Susan, temporarily caught off guard. Vitamin shots made sense and explained the boost in his appearance. Hopefully, the shots would boost things in other areas too. "Well, good. I'm glad you're taking steps to address things."

"Yes. Come here, Mrs. Durham." Jerome reached out and pulled her close.

As always, the touch of his hands made her catch her breath. She hated to do it, but she picked up his hands with her own and removed them from her waist. She frowned on personal displays of affection in the office and strictly enforced her own rules.

"While I was down there, they drew some blood. Just to check things out," he said, casually.

"Okay," Susan said. She patted his shoulder and looked at him.

"Those test results will be back in a few days, but the doctor scheduled me to go in and have some other tests."

"What other tests, Jerome?" The first edge of concern crept into Susan's voice. "Tests for what?"

"Well, I'm sure you've noticed that my weight's down a bit. I've been more tired lately, and you know I've been having these headaches," Jerome said. "I think it's just this rigorous campaign schedule. I'm an older man now, and I know my body has to adjust." He looked into his wife's eyes. "But the doctor wants to be certain everything is all right. As your next mayor, I must say I tend to agree with him."

Susan took a deep breath and exhaled. Jerome seemed confident and relaxed so she would be too.

"When is your appointment?" she said.

He smiled. "Next week."

"Then I'll be there."

❧ CHAPTER 4 ☙

Trudy Durham stood at the stove in her kitchen, trying to think of a way to bring up a sore topic with her husband, Carl. She was contemplating volunteering for Jerome's mayoral campaign. Of her two sisters-in-law, Trudy was the one Susan would have preferred to have working down at headquarters, since she had useful skills as an accountant, was well-mannered, and was already a prim dresser who wouldn't need to be told how to act or what to wear.

In reality, Trudy was too busy to even consider volunteering for Jerome. When she wasn't working at her part-time job, she might be tied up with any one of the many various church clubs, committees, and other organizations she was involved with. Trudy signed up for anything and everything that the church had going on. She didn't realize it, but her sisters-in-law knew that Trudy had gotten involved with the Mount Zion Missionary Baptist Church in an attempt to endear herself to her husband's mother, Hattie Durham. Mother Durham had been nice enough to Trudy, but it seemed to Trudy that her mother-in-law mostly ignored her.

The situation was confusing to Trudy. Mother Durham had made no bones about the fact that she disliked Susan, who – in her mind – had "ambushed" Jerome into marriage, adding insult to injury by convincing him to elope, depriving her of the chance to see her favorite son walk down the aisle. There didn't seem to be a thing Susan could do right as far as Hattie was concerned, and the old woman had often alluded to some sort of mysterious trouble that Susan had dragged Jerome into when they first met, requiring Hattie to come to the rescue.

"If it wasn't for me you wouldn't be here right now sitting up on that high yellow horse of yours," Trudy had heard Hattie mutter, many a time. "Hussy."

Then, there was Donetta, who had caused a scandal for the family by being twenty years younger than Junior, and getting pregnant by him before they were married and before he was legally divorced from his wife at the time.

Trudy had thought she would fit right into place as the "good" daughter-in-law, but Hattie seemed to barely notice her. Instead, she seemed to prefer Donetta, whose lively personality seemed to win everyone over.

Trudy thought getting involved in the church Hattie loved so much would bring her and her mother-in-law closer. They would get to spend more time together, and Hattie would see how good Trudy was for her middle son, Carl. So, Trudy joined the choir and the Women's Mission, sat on the board of the Baptist Training Union, and volunteered as an usher. She became a Sunday school teacher and an alternate van driver for the youth program. On top of that, she was the church treasurer and worked part time in the accounting office.

Still, Trudy had thought she might find some time to help out with Jerome's mayoral campaign. She bounced the idea off her husband, Carl. Carl was the second of Hattie Durham's three sons, and he looked the most like their deceased father, Lewis. Carl was shorter than his two brothers, though still well built and muscular.

"What do you think about me helping out on your brother's campaign?" Trudy asked.

"Trudy, girl, when do you got time for that?" Carl said.

"Well, I know I couldn't work any kind of regular hours, but I could hand out flyers at rallies or just go in every once in awhile and lend an extra hand down there," she added.

"Girl, you're crazy," Carl declared. He downed his Scotch. "Besides, Jerome don't need no more help. I heard he has so many young girls working down there they don't even have chairs for everyone."

"I'd be happy to take my own chair," Trudy laughed, trying to lighten her husband's mood. "And I thought since Donetta's helping out down there too ..."

Carl snorted. "What else Donetta got to do? She don't work. You do. And that's on top of a hundred and one other things you got to do, since you belong to everything they got going on up at the church."

"Well, I just wanted to try to do something to help your brother become our city's next mayor," Trudy said.

She watched Carl pour himself another shot. He started to drink it, looked up, and caught the disappointed look on her face.

"Do you know you are just like my Mama?" Carl looked at her with disgust. "Dancing around like a puppet on a string for Jerome. All of y'all." He downed his second drink, slammed the glass down on the table, and left the room.

Trudy sat there. She really was disappointed in not to be able to help out much with the campaign; Carl was right about that. But this was not about catering to Jerome; she really wanted to take part in things.

These days, she felt she especially could have used the companionship of her two sisters-in-law. It would be nice to have other women around to talk to. Donetta and Susan were both married to Durham men and maybe they would have some advice on the changes in her Durham man.

Carl wasn't normally so bad-tempered. But he had not been himself for the past several years, she thought. Since his mother, Hattie, passed, Carl had grown increasingly sullen and withdrawn. Trudy had heard stories about the kind of man his father Lewis had been, and it seemed like Carl was deliberately becoming more and more like him: drinking, gambling, and staying out all hours of the night.

Trudy took solace in her work and her many church activities. It kept her mind occupied and often kept her out of Carl's angry presence as well. But his behavior was starting to trouble her. His childish jealousy over Jerome being the favorite was just another source of his anger.

Trudy knew Lewis Durham, Sr., had often taken his fists to his wife, so Trudy now found herself watching his son Carl with a cautious eye. Over the years, Trudy had put up with a lot from Carl, but he had never hit her, and she had never been afraid that he would, until recently.

Trudy made herself a promise. "If he ever does raise

his hand to me, I'll leave him," she whispered.

The thought made her so nervous she could hardly stand. After all these years, how could she make it out in this world, all alone? She prayed she would never have to find out.

CHAPTER 5

Trudy decided there was something she could do after all to help Jerome's campaign, and it would take little more than an hour's time out of her morning. She called Reverend Solomon and asked if the church would be willing to lend a half dozen folding chairs to Jerome Durham's campaign. This church as well as other black churches in the area and throughout the state formed the basis of support for Councilman Durham. Having grown up in their bosom, Jerome was their native son. As a group, they had specifically chosen him as the representative they would support going forward, giving him a beautiful gold signet ring to pledge their loyalty to him. Trudy knew the reverend would say yes, and he did, helping her load the chairs into the back of the church van so she could drop them off at Durham for Mayor HQ.

Trudy came to a stop at the corner of an intersection in a fairly busy retail and business zone. She did a double-take as she saw a tall man ushering an almost equally tall woman into the restaurant at the corner. Junior! That was her brother-in-law, Lewis, Jr., Trudy was sure of it. She had only seen him for a second, and, by the time she looked back at him, he had opened the door and entered the restaurant, but she would know the walk of a Durham brother anywhere – all three of them walked that way. *That was Junior,* she thought. *So, who was that lady with him?*

Trudy shook her head as she drove carefully on. Carl's brother had a reputation as a lady killer and being married for the third time didn't seem to have changed that at all. Trudy couldn't help wondering if Donetta knew the tall woman. All Trudy had seen of her was that she had on a nice dress, and it showed off her long, slender legs. Trudy herself stood all of five-four and had always wished her legs were longer, so she noticed that in other women. But she was too old to worry about that now, having had stumpy legs all of her life. Trudy chided herself now for thinking the worst of Junior. Her brother-in-law claimed to have settled down since he had met Donetta, and it was only right to believe her kin instead of the rumors from around town.

When Trudy arrived at campaign headquarters, Donetta met her at the door with a few young men to unload the chairs.

"Hey, thank you, True. These are really gonna help out here," she said, greeting her little sister-in-law with a hug.

Trudy stood back and smiled. "Donetta, girl, you look wonderful," she said.

"Thank you for saying so. You know, I'm just trying to look the part, girl," Donetta responded. "Assistant to the next mayor of Sharon, Alabama."

"Amen to that," Trudy agreed. They laughed. "And is our proud power couple here? I'd love to say hello."

"Susan's in the office, but Jerome's not here. He still has his city council duties," Donetta said.

"Ok," said Trudy, rethinking seeing just Susan. Jerome was always pleasant, but conversations with Susan alone could sometimes be trying or awkward. She was saved by the voices of the twins yelling their "hellos" before running over to hug their Aunt True.

Carl and Trudy were childless, though she had badly wanted to have kids. She had never managed to get pregnant, and everyone assumed the problem was with her, as Carl was rumored to have fathered a couple of kids along the way somewhere. In his day, he had been as much of a playboy as his daddy was reputed to be, and – as the man's namesake – was still earning that reputation. Trudy was as good as a second mother to Jerome and Susan's boys, Roderick and Byron, when they were growing up, and now she filled that same role with Junior and Donetta's girls.

"You girls have grown three inches since I last saw you," said Trudy, opening her arms to both girls at once.

"That was just last week at Sunday school," Latasha pointed out.

"That doesn't mean it's not true," Trudy laughed. Talking about her lanky nieces' heights made her remember the tall woman who had been with Junior.

"Speaking of tall folk: Girls, how's your father?" Trudy said. She gave Donetta a meaningful look. "Since your mother hasn't said a word about him."

"Lewis, Jr., is just as fine as he ever was," Donetta said playfully. "I think he said he needed to talk to Carl about something, so you may run into him at your house. But if not, you'll see him at the party."

Trudy nodded. *If Donetta's concerned about Junior,*

she's not showing it, Trudy thought. She told the girls to be good, then told Donetta she had to be on her way. She also didn't mention anything more about saying a quick "hello" to Susan, and Donetta didn't bring it up.

Donetta walked Trudy back over to the van. "Oh, yeah, sis, and did I tell you that Susan and Jerome finally decided what they want to do for his birthday? We're all getting together at our house for dinner and drinks."

Trudy promised to bring her famous lasagna and fried chicken to the party, as well as some kind of dessert. She and Donetta shared their relief that the couple had opted for a family celebration. Donetta knew Susan had wanted to use her husband's birthday as a public and political activity, but Jerome had expressed his desire to be close to his family for the occasion.

The women were glad family was still the most important thing to their adored younger brother-in-law. Donetta loved entertaining. Spending time with his brothers always had a positive effect on Carl, so Trudy was especially looking forward to the occasion. It would also give her a chance to talk with Donetta privately about their mutual marital concerns.

"Be sure and thank Reverend Solomon, on behalf of everyone here, especially the councilman," said Donetta, giving Trudy a hearty farewell hug.

Driving away, Trudy had a big smile on her face. She was happy to have done something for Jerome. She also felt good after seeing and talking to Donetta, and she was glad she hadn't mentioned seeing Junior. Trudy would keep her eyes open, but she needed to know more before saying something to hurt her favorite sister-in-law.

CHAPTER 6

Carl Durham's business partners, Deke Baker and Otis Johnson, were his ace buddies as well. Hattie Durham's father had raised a second family with a woman named Bessie who lived just down the road from where he kept Hattie's mother and her siblings. Though Hattie had known her generous mother to help Bessie and her kids out with food or money from time to time, for the most part, the females from the two families ignored each other and even talked behind each other's backs. But the boys in the family had no such compunctions. They hung out and played together, and, years later as adults, Carl remained good friends with Deke, who was the offspring of one of those distant half cousins. Otis Johnson was the son of Hattie's second husband, Charlie. The first initials of the three friends formed the name of their garage, CDOs, and up until now it had done very well. But Deke and Otis noticed a change in Carl recently and had begun accusing him of slacking off. Carl got the family's approval to invite the two men to Jerome's birthday party. He hoped that the relaxed occasion would put them at ease and get them to back off a bit.

It turned out to be quite a party. Junior and Donetta provided ribs, steaks, potato salad, green bean casserole, and liquor. Donetta also baked her famous lemon swirl pound cake, which was the guest of honor's favorite. Trudy brought the food she had promised, plus a couple of sweet potato pies and a big tossed salad. Even Susan got in on the cooking action, showing up with a dish of steamed vegetables and a delicious shrimp étouffée. Though the family rarely got to see it, Susan was a skilled cook who had learned her way around the kitchen from the woman who had raised her as a child in Louisiana.

The twins were allowed to have some friends over and a handful of teenaged boys had already showed up. Donetta wondered if her daughters had even asked any other girls to come. Susan and Jerome were sitting on the couch, watching the two older Durham brothers deal cards. They were showing the youngsters how to play poker.

The doorbell rang, and Donetta went to answer it. It was Gloria Ricks, a woman who was new to the neighborhood but who had wasted no time getting acquainted with everyone in it. Especially the men.

"Hi, girl!" Gloria said brightly.

Donetta's smile was polite. "Hello, Gloria. What can I do for you this evening?"

"Oh, I just stopped by to borrow a mixing bowl." Gloria craned her neck, trying to see what was going on in the house. "I thought I would bake a cake, but a lot of my nice kitchenware is still boxed up, and I didn't feel like unpacking everything trying to find it. Are you all having a party?"

Donetta was pretty sure she had mentioned it earlier that day when Gloria had stopped by to borrow some pliers from Junior. She and Junior had been sniffing around each other ever since Gloria had arrived in the neighborhood, and Donetta could not believe how brazen the woman was.

"Mama, who's at the door?" Latasha called. She was waiting for a young man she had invited. Gloria used the distraction to squeeze past Donetta into the house.

"It's just me, honey," Gloria announced, loudly enough so that everyone looked up and saw her standing there. Too tight was the only description for her outfit. "I just came to borrow a bowl, so I can bake a cake. I see you all have a beautiful cake on the table. Must be someone's birthday? Donetta, did you bake that? It smells delicious."

"It's my birthday," said Jerome, offering his charming smile. "Would you like to have some, Miss ... ?"

"Ricks, Gloria Ricks." Gloria shook his hand and beamed up at him. "Councilman Durham, you don't need any introduction. I've seen you about a million times on TV."

Donetta shook her head. Just like that, Gloria had weaseled her way into the party. Donetta decided she wasn't going to let it bother her. Junior didn't seem particularly worried about Gloria, but then he had always been cucumber cool when it came to his wife and the women he was messing around with. Now that she thought about it, Donetta realized that things seemed to have cooled down between those two over the past couple of weeks. Gloria was focusing instead on Jerome.

"Oooh, Donetta," Gloria squealed. Her eyes were on Jerome as she placed a piece of cake in her mouth, and slowly licked her lips and fingertips. "This cake is truly divine. Can I get the recipe?"

Jerome looked embarrassed and turned to his wife. "Susan, can I get you something to drink?"

Susan shook her head and patted his thigh. She was suffering through the evening for his benefit and couldn't wait to go home. Gloria Ricks was annoying, but Susan had endured worse. She turned her head, refusing to watch the woman's attempt to make cake consumption into a pornographic act.

Moving back and forth between the kitchen and the living room, cleaning up as she went along, Trudy saw the expressions on both Susan's and Donetta's faces; Susan was clearly bored, but Donetta was watching Gloria Ricks intently. Trudy thought she could guess the reason why: Junior's reputation was well known.

Donetta caught Trudy's eye and quickly looked away. She knew what her sister-in-law was thinking. Trudy felt like turnabout was fair play when it came to Junior's infidelity, since he had been married with children when he got Donetta pregnant.

Donetta supposed that was fair. But she and Junior had talked about it many times. He had sworn to her that she was different, that he had learned his lesson, and that she was the only woman in the world that mattered to him and that he truly wanted to share his life with. She wanted to believe him. He looked her way and smiled the biggest, most open smile in the world. There was no guilt whatsoever in that smile, as if he had nothing in the world to hide.

Looking at Gloria now, Donetta's confidence came flooding back. Even if Junior was messing with Gloria, the woman would not be able to hold his interest for long.

She might be good at stuffing herself into a tight skirt, but she was neither clever nor that interesting when it came down to it. There was nothing really special about Gloria Ricks. She wasn't even that attractive. Whatever had been between her and Junior seemed to be over now. It was likely that the woman had just used Junior to get close to his brother, the councilman, anyway. It wouldn't be the first time that had happened. Donetta smiled back at Junior.

Trudy came over and stood by Donetta to watch the show. Trudy wondered if she should say anything about what she had seen that morning and thought better of it. Donetta hadn't seemed that worried about Gloria Ricks, just curious and maybe a little mad. But the woman Trudy had seen Junior with was something else. Even though she had only caught a glimpse of her from the back, Trudy could tell she was no ordinary neighborhood homewrecker. Judging from her car and clothes, the woman had expensive taste and the money to indulge it – she clearly had class. With Donetta running around trying so hard to impress and fit in with Susan and Jerome, she did not need anything to add to her insecurities. Trudy chided herself for even thinking of hurting Donetta that way. She vowed to keep the information to herself until the time was right.

Gloria was overdoing it, squeezing her way down onto the couch between Lashonna and Jerome, while Susan watched with a frozen smile.

"She oughta be used to that by now," Trudy remarked. "Susan, I mean."

"Oh, she is," Donetta said. "You should see him

down at headquarters. Women are all over him all the time. That's one of the reasons he wanted a private party with mainly just the family. Don't worry; Rome can handle himself."

"Oh, I know he can," Trudy said, "but Gloria might want to watch out for the councilman's wife tonight. I don't think Susan is in the mood for this tonight."

"You know, you're right," Donetta said. "Time to break this shit up."

She clapped her hands and called her daughters to her side. The three of them slipped out of the room and then returned wearing huge starched wigs and false eyelashes.

Susan still sat straight-backed on the sofa, her face motionless. Trudy might have thought she was vexed by the woman flirting with Jerome, but that was the furthest thing from her mind. Not only was she used to tarts trying to pull Jerome, she was confident that they could not succeed. Jerome was a faithful man.

Susan was worried that Jerome would want her to get up with him and perform one of the duets they had practiced in their living room. It was one thing to play Teena Marie to Jerome's Rick James and sing "Fire and Desire" in front of the mirrored wall in the privacy of their own home. Here in front of the family, it suddenly seemed ridiculous. She was sure she could not go through with it.

"Karaoke time!" Donetta announced. Latasha whispered to one of the boys, who went to the front of the room with a grand gesture. She and her sister lined up behind her mother.

"Councilman Durham, in honor of your birthday,

these ladies would like to honor you with a song prepared especially for you. Ladies and gentleman, presenting Diana Ross and the Supremes!" Donetta said.

After the brief introduction, Donetta and her twin girls started the evening's show lip syncing "Ain't No Mountain High Enough." After they were done, the boys started beatboxing and performed a freestyle rap. The adults agreed they were pretty good, and Latasha and Lashonna behaved as though they were superstars, screaming and yelling at the front of the room. As their performance ended, Donetta pulled the one uninvited guest aside.

"Gloria, we've kept you far too long," Donetta said. She hadn't said anything earlier because she didn't want to seem rude, but now it was time for Ms. Ricks to go.

"Oh, okay," Gloria said. She was clearly disappointed. She scrambled up, then turned back around with a wide smile. She had an idea.

"All of you ladies and gentlemen have put on a great show here tonight. But now, I'd like to sing for the councilman, too!" She went over to the teenagers, who were bending over Junior and Donetta's record collection. "Do you have that song 'Ring My Bell' in there, baby?"

Before Donetta could protest, Gloria sashayed to the middle of the floor as the fast, disco era song began to play. "The backup part is easy, girls. Jump in and help me. Donetta and Trudy, you can jump in too."

Donetta and Trudy stayed put, but Gloria wouldn't have noticed anyway. She was fully involved in her wholehearted, rump-shaking performance, swinging her backside in fast time with the music. She kept turning around to give her audience a good look as she wiggled and shook shamelessly, looking over her shoulder to see if she had their full attention. She mainly seemed interested in Jerome's attention. The girls giggled behind their hands, but the woman's performance had the boys riveted until the end. None of them had ever seen a grown woman behave in quite that way.

"All right, all right now," Gloria was breathless as she accepted the polite applause from the women in the room and the more enthusiastic applause from Deke, Otis, and the twins' friends. Jerome and Junior saw their wives' faces and clapped politely, maintaining what they hoped were stoic, husbandly expressions.

"Well, thank you, Gloria. You can be going now," said Donetta, handing Gloria the mixing bowl. Donetta's relief at finally getting rid of Gloria was short-lived: Junior jumped up ready for his turn on the floor, and Gloria's eyes lit up at the chance of getting to see the councilman perform.

"Oh, I gotta stay for this, Donetta," said Gloria, evading the hostess smoothly. She turned back into the living room. "Me and the boys, and you and your girls, performed for the men, and now it's their turn to perform for us. I don't want to miss this."

The Durham brothers – all three of them – were notorious hams, and there was no way Junior was going to let a bunch of women and children outdo him at a talent show. He motioned to the kids to locate his favorite Temptations recording, and he urged Carl and Jerome to get up with him. Susan gave Jerome a look that held him in his seat initially as the opening strains of "Can't Get Next to You" filled the room. Deke and Otis joined in. They urged the youngsters to participate. The boys were embarrassed and hung back at first, but then they seemed to get into it.

The family had seen this routine many times, and it never failed to entertain all who were present. Even Susan got into it as the men harmonized along with the record. Laughing, Jerome could not resist standing up to join the other men. Like his brothers, he had a pretty good singing voice and moved gracefully. The women whooped and hollered for the beautiful black men dancing in front of them. Jerome confidently tried to execute a classic move: a big step forward, a dip and a wave, a glide backward and spin. As he pivoted, Jerome's head began spinning for real. He lost his balance and crashed to the floor.

As he swam in and out of consciousness, Jerome heard and saw bits and flashes of what was going on around him.

"Brother!"

"Uncle Jerome!"

"Jerome, can you hear me?"

"Everybody, get back and give him room to breathe, for goodness' sake!"

That was his wife, Susan, and he could see her pale, concerned face hovering over him. Gloria Ricks was running around, craning her neck trying to see him and getting in the way.

"Unbutton his shirt, so he can get some air," Gloria suggested. She made the mistake of reaching for his collar herself, but Susan barred her with her arm.

"I said, get back! Lashonna, please get your uncle some water," Susan said.

Lashonna's eyes grew wide at the brewing altercation between Susan and Gloria. Jerome saw his niece run from the room. He tried to speak, but no sound came out. Gloria backed off.

"Gloria, you need to go on home now," Donetta said. She turned her attention back to her brother in law as Gloria hung around, trying to hide in the background behind the men.

What a shame to see a fine man like Jerome Durham fall out like that, Gloria thought. She didn't mind seeing him laid out full length on the ground, though, as it put his lean physique on display. The councilman was nicely built.

"Jerome, are you all right?" Susan reached for Jerome's hand. She felt for his pulse and leaned her head against his chest.

"My god, honey, your heart is racing," Jerome heard her say, as her face went out of focus again. The room was in chaos.

"He needs an ambulance," Susan said, and she was surprised at how steady and calm her voice was. Her own heart was pounding. "Someone, please call for an ambulance."

Donetta had already picked up the phone. Trudy stood with a cushion for Jerome's head, but Susan cradled him in her lap. She continued to issue orders.

"Latasha, please bring our coats so we'll be ready to go when they get here. Would someone hand me my purse?" Jerome stared into Susan's eyes, willing her to read his mind. As a couple, they had always been in sync. Susan looked at Jerome and nodded, then gestured for Junior to come close.

"Lewis, would you please get Gloria out of here, and make sure she keeps quiet about this?" she hissed. "No one can know about us rushing Jerome to the hospital tonight. I'm sure it's nothing, anyway, but this is a private family matter."

Junior nodded and went to deal with Gloria as Susan turned back to soothe Jerome.

Donetta saw her husband ushering Gloria out. *The nerve of that heifer to still be here when I told her to get out*, Donetta thought. She followed long enough to shove the mixing bowl into Gloria's hands, as the woman had put it down on a table then forgotten all about it.

Trudy helpfully ushered the children out of the room as the sound of an ambulance came into earshot. Susan called Carl over.

"I'm sure there are going to be some nosy neighbors out there," Susan said. "I don't think anyone will be able to see who's on the stretcher because it's so dark, but some folks around here probably know Jerome is related to the homeowners, and they might even know Lewis and Donetta were hosting this party here tonight. Will you and Otis and Deke stand out there and make sure that nobody says anything?"

"Anything you say, Susie," Carl answered. For once he sounded sincere while talking to her, even though he had called her by that hated nickname.

"Thank you," she said evenly. For a moment the two looked at one another, and each saw fear in the other's face. Their differences didn't matter at that moment; they both loved Jerome. Carl gathered his bewildered friends, and they donned coats and went outside, grateful to have something to do.

The EMTs came in and got Jerome loaded on a stretcher. Susan gave Donetta the keys to her car so that she could drive it over to the hospital. The men would be there, and she would ride home with her husband. Trudy clasped Susan's hands with her own and gave her a hug.

"You know we are all praying for our brother," Trudy said. "We love Jerome, and the Lord loves him too, and he is going to be fine."

Susan nodded numbly and allowed Junior to help her into the ambulance. Jerome's vital signs had stabilized by the time they reached the hospital. He was able to sit up and tell the doctors about the tests he was already scheduled for. They decided to keep Jerome overnight for observation.

A plump nurse with a pretty brown face came in and started adjusting the IV drip. She explained that they were going to give him some fluids, because he was slightly dehydrated and showed signs of anemia as well.

"He's been getting vitamin injections lately too to help keep his energy up," Susan said. "His schedule is so hectic. He might have missed the last couple of weeks."

"Don't you worry. We'll fatten this man of yours right up!" the nurse said.

The pretty nurse saw that her humor was lost on the councilman's wife, whose expression remained serious as she excused herself from the room.

Susan waited outside for the nurse to come out.

"Nurse, thank you for taking care of my husband," she said. "I'll ask you personally not to talk to anyone about his visit here tonight. His office will issue a statement, if necessary."

"It's my job to honor patient privacy," Nurse Jones said. Her voice and expression were neutral.

"Thank you," Susan said crisply. "It's just that he's running for mayor, as you know, and we don't need people trying to use this against him."

What am I doing? Susan thought. *I don't have to explain myself to this nurse.* But though an around-the-way girl like this probably would keep quiet at the hospital, she would probably think nothing at all of mentioning to her family and friends that Jerome Durham had come to the hospital that night. People like that always seemed to feel familiar with Jerome and treated him like something they owned. Jerome cultivated their sentiment for political purposes, but it could be dangerous in a situation like this. The trick was to use that loyalty to their advantage. She thought she had done a good job of it, since Nurse Jones was nodding empathetically.

"Me and my husband were at his last rally," Nurse Jones said. "And I can tell the man works hard. Do you know I tried to get one of those autographed pictures they were giving away, but we couldn't get close to any of the booths, it was so crowded."

"Write your address down, and I'll have someone send you one," said Susan, smiling sweetly. "What's your husband's name? The councilman will personalize it."

"Really?" Nurse Jones beamed. She wasted no time in scribbling her information on a notepad and handing it to Susan. "Oh, thank you so much. My husband's name is Bubba. Have him write it out to Mr. & Mrs. Bubba Jones." She thought for a moment. "On second thought, just have him write it out to me. 'With love, to Jeanette Jones.' Bubba wasn't here!"

"Thank you again," Susan said. She felt worn out suddenly. The night had caught up with her.

Nurse Jones patted her shoulder. "You go home and get a good night's rest, Mrs. Durham, and leave the councilman to us. He'll be ready to go, shipshape, in the morning."

Susan drove home alone in her Mercedes sedan. She had turned down the family's offers to drive her, but they insisted on following her to make sure she got home okay. Donetta had wanted to ride with her, as a precaution, but Susan managed to discourage that idea, to her own great relief. She needed the time to catch her breath and think. She resisted the terror that threatened to grip her over Jerome's condition. The hospital said he seemed fine, just dehydrated and fatigued. Susan needed to put her mind to work as to how they could keep up with Jerome's stepped-up appearance schedule without literally exhausting the man. She pulled up in her driveway and flashed her lights to let the others know she was all right. They hovered until she had opened the front door and blinked the porch light as well. She appreciated their concern, but she was relieved when they left. She wanted to be alone with her thoughts. Whatever was wrong with Jerome, he needed to get over it fast.

She walked into the house, lingering in the hallway just long enough to hang up her coat. She paused in the living room entranceway and scanned the photographs on the mantelpiece. It was the usual lineup, consisting of some recent portraits of her and Jerome, pictures of their sons, others of Carl and Junior with their families, and, of course, the handsomely framed portrait photo of Hattie Durham. Susan's eyes stopped there. How proud Hattie had been of the expensive new hat and suit she had worn that day, gifts from her favorite son, Jerome. The old woman's lively eyes seemed to stare right from the portrait into Susan's own.

She stood there entranced for a moment, then shook her head and turned to head up the stairs. She regretted ever going into the living room, but she had felt drawn there. It was as if she had needed to tell Hattie about Jerome being in the hospital. Not to worry, Mother Durham, your baby boy is gonna be just fine.

CHAPTER 7

When Jerome woke up in the hospital the next morning, it took him a moment to remember where he was and why, but he actually felt good as new. He told Susan so as he straightened the collar of the fresh shirt she had brought for him to put on, and he even suggested that they stop by the church on their way home. Jerome had been scheduled to make a few remarks that morning, but Susan absolutely refused to take any chances with his health. She had already asked Junior to stand up on his brother's behalf at the church. The doctor came in to speak with them before they left.

"I'm glad to see you're feeling better this morning, Mr. Durham," she said formally.

"It was nothing but a momentary dizzy spell," Jerome replied. "I've been really busy lately. I think it all finally caught up to me."

"Yes, I'm sure that is true. I'm glad we kept you here for observation," the doctor responded. "You mentioned that your primary physician had already run some tests, so we called over. The results were expedited and sent over immediately."

Susan felt a sudden panic. Jerome reached for her hand.

"Dr. Mathieson wanted to be here to discuss this with

you, but he couldn't make it today. However, we thought it would be best for us to inform you that there are some concerns with your test results."

Jerome frowned. "What sort of concerns, doctor?"

"There are some abnormalities in the bloodwork," the doctor said.

"What could it possibly be?"

"Without going into details, Mr. Durham, there are many different possibilities with as many different treatment options."

"Is it serious?"

"I don't want to alarm you," the doctor said. "I just want to caution you to be proactive, and get the rest you need today. Dr. Mathieson will see you and give you more details tomorrow, but we needed to let you know because he wants you on immediate bed rest."

"I feel fine," Jerome said. "And I have too much to do."

Susan exchanged glances with the doctor.

"It's Sunday, honey," she cajoled. "I'm sure it won't be too hard to take it easy for the rest of the day. We can talk to your doctor tomorrow, and he can tell us what's up then."

The couple stifled their anxieties and checked out. They filled a prescription for Jerome at the pharmacy and said little on the way home. Susan knew better than to bring it up. Her husband was a stubborn man who believed he was invincible. He had told her that he had once been deathly ill as a boy, but had not been really ill a day in his life since recovering from diphtheria. His mother Hattie told that story to anyone who would listen, claiming that she had both "prayed and paid" for special protection over his health. Jerome was not about to entertain the thought of having a serious illness.

Once they got home, Susan made her husband put his feet up, brought him some coffee and a fruit platter, and anxiously hovered over him as they discussed his campaign plans for the next few weeks.

Usually, Susan appeared along with Jerome at events, or saw to his other business while he fulfilled his commitments, but now she suggested splitting his appearances up between them just as a way to keep his life from being quite so hectic.

"Nobody's saying you're sick, Jerome," she reassured him. "But you said yourself that you've been tired and run down lately. Let's figure out how to keep you from spreading yourself too thin." She assured Jerome that Donetta could easily take on more responsibility supervising the staff at HQ, while his city council staff would stay on top of things at his city office.

Susan relished the idea of expanding her role in Jerome's push for the mayor's office. She had long felt capable of being more than just a glorified campaign manager, and she was sure her increased visibility would only enhance his candidacy. Everybody always talked about how poised and well-spoken she was, not to mention how beautiful. People would see that Jerome Durham's wife was more than just his helpmeet: she was a true partner in his vision and leadership of their fair city. Excited, she began to plan a whole new wardrobe.

After church, Donetta called to see how Jerome was doing.

"He's fine. He's resting now," Susan said. Her tone was

a bit impatient. "How did it go with Junior at church?"

"It went just fine. You know that man loves to hear the sound of his own voice, so he was in hog heaven once he got that microphone in his face," Donetta said and laughed in her playful way.

Susan remained serious. "Did he mention Jerome's jobs plans or say anything about Ted Lawson's failure to respond to the church's invitation?"

"No, he just kept it simple," Donetta replied. She couldn't understand why Susan was so worked up. "He just apologized on Jerome's behalf and thanked the church. He told the congregation that Rome would probably be back next week or the week after that. I told him to keep that part of it vague since we didn't know for sure when he could make it."

"Good, good," Susan said. Her mind was whirring. A thought came to her mind, and she panicked. "He didn't say why Jerome wasn't there, did he?"

"No, no," Donetta soothed her. "Junior just said Jerome had something come up that couldn't wait, and that he knew the church would understand. Which, of course, they did. Everybody knows what an important man he is, and they all love him, besides. And they still took up a special collection to donate to his campaign."

Satisfied, Susan told Donetta she had to go look after Jerome but she would see her at the office first thing in the morning. Upstairs, to her surprise, Jerome was resting just as she had admonished him to. He had positioned himself amidst a bunch of papers on their bed.

Now he was sitting up on the bed, propped up on his

pillows, with his papers still spread out around him. It didn't look like he had done much reading, though; in fact, he was dozing off. Susan stifled the urge to fuss and began stacking up his work. He came alert as he felt her gently pushing him down by the shoulders into more of a lying-down position.

"Quiet, honey," Susan soothed. "I'll sort through all of this stuff and brief you on it later, just like we discussed. That way you don't have to worry about all the fussy little details. You go on and have a nice nap. Lunch will be ready when you wake up."

Jerome grabbed his wife by the waist and pulled her in close for a kiss. "You're so good to me," he said. "I don't know what I would do without you."

"Thank goodness, you'll never have to find out," she teased, chucking his chin and kissing him back. Jerome leaned back and closed his eyes, able to relax knowing that she was near and taking care of things.

The couple's ability to rely on one another without hesitation was the basis of their marriage. Years ago, Jerome had promised to protect Susan from answering any questions in the death of her former fiancé, Chancelly Foster, and he had done just that, enlisting his mother's help in covering the truth. Since that day, he'd been Susan's hero and protector. Now it was her turn to help and protect him, and she relished the chance.

Susan shook her hair loose and curled up on the settee with Jerome's files in front of her. She made quick work of organizing things into appropriate piles, and then settled back with the most important things. As she went through the pages, she made a list of the various calls her husband needed to make, and another of the people and places that required an actual visit. From that list, Susan figured she could represent her husband on most of the calls and more than half of the personal visits. A whole lot of things merely required an administrative call, which Donetta or someone else at the office could handle.

Then she made notes of her opinion on things that required a decision or comment from Jerome. They could talk through those items later, when he woke up. Cutting through the pile of busywork Jerome had planned to take on himself, it struck Susan that not only did she enjoy the work, she was good at it.

She smiled with confidence as she thought about Jerome's campaign. She would take care of things for as long as he needed. Jerome would be able to rest and focus on getting well, knowing that she had his back. When he was healthy and back at 100 percent, he would be able to return to his work without skipping a beat. Thanks to her smooth handling, no one would ever notice he'd been gone.

CHAPTER 8

Lewis Durham, Jr., entered the offices of Hickland, Travis and Epperson. A tall, attractive man with a flirtatious personality, Lewis exuded professionalism in a sharp brown suit. He nodded his head as he looked around, impressed with the expensive décor. He had met with Beverly Epperson several times, but never at her office. She was always so busy that it was usually easier for her to meet with him between appointments, on her way to somewhere. They had gotten together at restaurants, the library, or even the park, but today was a rare occasion.

The receptionist was a young thing who tried her best to flirt with him without breaking her own professionalism. "Miss Epperson will be right with you, Mr. Durham," she said, offering him her loveliest smile. "Why don't you have a seat, and I'll get you something to drink."

Junior nodded politely, watching her as she stood up from her desk and went over to a counter with a sink and coffee pot. A small refrigerator was positioned under the counter. She turned to him, striking a pretty pose. She wore a very short skirt.

"Would you prefer coffee or a soda?" she asked sweetly.

Junior noticed that she hadn't attempted to notify

Beverly that he was there yet. This girl was flirting with him all right. He cleared his throat. "Umm, soda, please. It's pretty hot out there." *And in here, too*, he thought.

She bent over to open the fridge. Being the ladies' man that he was, Junior couldn't help appreciating the view. The girl stood up with a can in each hand.

"Do you like cola or would you rather have something clear?" she asked brightly.

"If you have some cold water, I'd better have that," he said. He could hear Donetta now, telling him that he didn't need the sugar. Of any kind. He watched as the receptionist bent back over to retrieve a bottle of water from the fridge and smiled gratefully at her as she walked over and handed to him.

He opened it and took a long swig. The water was ice cold, and he definitely needed to cool off. Before she got back to her desk, one of the carved wooden office doors swung open and Beverly Epperson emerged.

"There you are, Mr. Durham," she said. "I thought you were late. I was just coming out to see if you
had called."

"I was just getting Mr. Durham something to drink," the receptionist said. "I was getting ready to buzz you."

Beverly gave her a dubious look, then gestured to Junior. "Come on in," she said, heading back into her office before he had a chance to stand up. "We have a lot to talk about."

Junior nodded to the receptionist and followed Beverly into her office, water bottle in hand. He stood in the entrance, looking around.

"This is nice," he said. "Congratulations on the promotion, Beverly."

Already seated at her desk, she looked up at the man who practically filled her doorway with his height and shoulders. Lewis Durham, Jr., was a good-looking man. No wonder the girl out front had taken her time seeing him in.

"Please have a seat, Mr. Durham," Beverly said, indicating the chair in front of her. "Lewis."

They exchanged a conspiratorial smile. They had agreed to address each other formally when anyone else was present, but to use first names when they were alone. They had been working together for a while and were developing a mutually comfortable working relationship.

Beverly Epperson was an impressive young woman. She had just made partner at the firm, and Junior had passed by a painter adding her name to the sign out front that previously read "Brickman and Travis." Beverly was a good lawyer who worked diligently on all of her cases, but Junior knew his case was especially important to her. Now that she had made partner, she was under even more pressure to prove her worth to the firm, and the Durham name was big in this town. Beverly knew she had better have her act together if she planned on bringing legal charges or any trouble whatsoever to Susan Durham's door.

"Lewis, I want to review a few details before we decide on the next step," she said.

"Whatever you say, Beverly." Junior was agreeable. "Why don't we sit on the sofa? We can be more comfortable there," she suggested, and got up with a sheaf of papers in her hand. She spread them out on the wide oak coffee table and sat down gracefully on the small leather loveseat.

Junior straightened his tie and joined her, making an effort not to stare at her crossed legs. Beverly Epperson was almost as tall as he was, and her long, toned legs were one of her best features. She often emphasized them by wearing short skirts and high heels, but she downplayed the rest of her looks. She wore very little makeup, kept her hair pulled back, and hid her face behind a pair of blocky glasses. But Junior, who considered himself a connoisseur when it came to females, recognized the beauty behind the Plain Jane act.

"All right, let's go through the facts one more time," said Beverly, completely focused on work now. "First of all, nothing much has changed here. We still have an uphill battle, because your family signed waivers when they requested that your mother be brought to your brother's home while on that respirator."

"The hospital never should have agreed to that, but Jerome and Susan muscled them into it," Junior said.

"We could still make a wrongful death claim against the manufacturer, citing faulty equipment," Beverly said. "But they say the machine was in good working condition, and, if we sue, they'll push their argument that the machine was purposely disabled." She looked at him grimly. "But you're not interested in suing the manufacturer, right?"

"That's right," Junior said. "Although, if that's the way to bring the idea that the machine was purposely disabled to somebody's attention, I might consider it."

"That would be a costly way to go about it," she said. "And now, so many years later, that would definitely be hard to prove. Unless there was a witness or actual videotape of the incident, it would just be speculation, and speculation won't do much for us at this point."

"Well, the circumstances surrounding the equipment malfunction are still as fishy as they ever were," Junior said. "No one can deny that."

"That's true," Beverly said. "We have the nurse's statement that your sister-in-law called her and told her not to come in that day, because there was a scheduling mistake and another nurse was coming in, right? But the nurse's agency claimed they never gave Susan Durham any such information, and the nurse was reprimanded for not verifying her schedule. She quit soon after, and we haven't been able to locate her to ask any more questions."

"Do we even need her anymore?" Junior asked. "If the agency has their written records, and as I understand it, they even have recordings of all of their incoming and outgoing phone calls that day?"

"It does look suspicious," she agreed. "But it's still just speculation."

"Well, what about the other nurse?" Junior persisted. "She said that Susan practically pushed her out of the house that day. She made her leave before her replacement arrived."

"Yes, and she was actually fired. Now she's afraid to say anymore because she does not want to lose her license to work because of that serious infraction. She won't talk to us anymore unless she's subpoenaed," Beverly said.

"Dammit," Junior growled. "I know Susan had something to do with this. I just know it. I feel it in my gut."

"Lewis, I understand your frustration but we've got to tread carefully here," Beverly said. She patted his hand.

"What excuses did she give again for lying to those nurses? What did she say her reasons were?" Junior asked.

"Her statement's not the most coherent thing I ever read, I must say," Beverly said. "First, she said she was confused about who she talked to on what day, because she was so upset. Later, when she was asked during the hospital investigation, she said she just wanted some peace and quiet because it had been so long since she had the house to herself. She didn't think a few minutes would hurt anything." Beverly rifled through her papers.

"A few minutes was all she needed," Junior said. "What was my brother thinking, leaving our mother alone with that woman?"

"He didn't leave them alone, remember?" Beverly said. "The nurse was still there."

"Well, what about the machine thing?" Junior said. "If we're back to that, how do we go about it? Do we have to bring a case against the manufacturer to get them to prove that the respirator wasn't faulty? Because if they prove that, doesn't that make the case that somebody deliberately turned the thing off so that my mother couldn't breathe? That somebody being my sister-in-law, Susan."

"I can look into it," Beverly said. "I think the testimony of the nurse's agency will lend credence to the fact that something was definitely going on, and if we present the case right, a judge might be willing to at least reopen the investigation."

She looked at him for a moment then continued. "So, what do you want me to do, Lewis? Should I draw up the papers and get the ball rolling?"

Junior sighed. He had waited a long time for this, wanting to give the family time to get over Ma'Dear's death before bringing this trouble to their door; once he accused Susan of murdering their mother, he would probably drive a wedge between the brothers that could never be removed, no matter the outcome of the case. Not to mention the pain it would cause Jerome. Junior sighed again.

"I still need time to think about this," he said. "Go ahead and get started with the paperwork, and I'll get back to you on what I want to do next."

The last few months had been harrowing. Dr. Mathieson's news that Jerome needed a bone marrow transplant sent the family reeling, but the Durham men had always stuck together. Without hesitation, Junior and Carl both volunteered to get tested for their cell compatibility with their younger brother.

"Don't worry, Jerome," Junior said. "One or the other of one of us is going to be your donor. You'll be back up on your feet in no time."

"That's right, boy," said Carl, ruffling his younger brother's shiny black hair.

Susan chewed her nails down to the quick every few days. She spent a lot of time in the nail salon but gave no other outward sign of her worry. Jerome continued to put on a brave face, and she did her best to follow her husband's example.

The two sat together in the hospital, anxiously consulting with Dr. Mathieson after the results of Carl's and Junior's blood tests were in.

"As I told you before, research has shown that the most successful potential match for this type of procedure is usually found in a compatible male family member with the same blood type and from the same paternal bloodline," the doctor explained. "With that in mind, the chances for a man such as yourself with two brothers are pretty good. But unfortunately, that is not the case here."

"What do you mean?" Jerome said. "All three of us have the same blood type. I know that from when my mother was in the hospital, we all had to be typed then."

The doctor looked up over his charts. He spoke carefully. "The bone marrow tests show that you do not share the paternal genetic markers with either of your brothers that would make them compatible donors for you." Dr. Mathieson paused and looked at Jerome directly before continuing. "Do you understand what I'm saying, Councilman Durham?"

"Wait a minute, doctor," Susan said. Jerome appeared to be in a daze. "Are you saying that Jerome doesn't have the same father as his two brothers?"

The doctor's expression was apologetic. "I'm afraid that is the case, Mrs. Durham." He looked at the two of them. "Listen, this is awkward news, and I'm sorry to be the one delivering it. It is an unfortunate distraction from the real matter at hand, which is to locate a suitable donor. Now, I understand that you two have sons?"

"My sons are not to be bothered with this," Jerome said firmly. "Is that understood?"

Jerome and Susan's sons, Roderick and Byron, were in their thirties. Both had successful military careers: Roderick in the Navy and Byron in the Air Force. Neither man was married, but Roddy had recently announced his intentions toward a Korean woman he had met on his latest tour of duty. Jerome was delighted by the news, as he relished the idea of having grandchildren. To her surprise, Susan found the idea even made her smile.

"Jerome, our sons have a right to know what's going on with their father," she said.

"We'll tell them once we have decided what we're going to do," he said. "When we come up with a plan that doesn't involve either of them being hospitalized, we can tell them everything."

"Neither one of them would be a match anyway," she said. It was both a relief and a disappointment. "They both have my blood type."

"While a family member is often the best match, it doesn't mean that they'd be the only match. Your information is being run against a database of potential other donors. We'll give it some time and see what happens. In the meantime, get some rest, Councilman Durham," said the doctor, closing his chart and leaving the room. The couple looked at each other.

"Oh, Jerome," Susan said. Her heart was in her throat as she turned to embrace him. He held her for a moment, letting the emotion soak in. Jerome simply wanted to comfort his wife. Drawing from his strength, Susan composed herself quickly.

"We're going to fight this thing, honey," she told him.

"Of course we are," he said. He smiled broadly, and his smile was real. "We're going to beat it. I've been feeling better, not worse, thanks to you. I wouldn't be surprised if they're wrong about the whole diagnosis, so we need to get a second opinion."

"We already have an appointment in a couple of days," she confirmed. She noticed a worried expression creeping over his features as he gathered their things.

"What is it, Jerome?" she inquired as he helped her

into her coat. She stopped him with a hand on his chin and looked into his eyes.

"We still have to tell my brothers that they're not compatible donors," he said. "Which means we have to tell them I had a different father than they did." There were tears in his eyes and a catch in his throat. "And I don't know who my real father is."

❦ CHAPTER 10 ❧

Seeing the state Jerome was in, Susan asked the nurse to give him a sedative. She assured him that they would deal with everything together later and reluctantly left his room so that he could sleep. Carl and Jerome were waiting outside, and she quickly pulled them into a waiting room for some privacy. She quietly gave them the news.

Lewis, Jr., and Carl were both stunned. Their reactions were similar to Jerome's. They each expressed denial, insisting that something had to be wrong with the tests and demanding that they go through the process again. Then, the slow realization kicked in about what their inability to donate cells to their younger brother really meant.

"You mean to say that me and Carl had a different daddy than Jerome," Junior repeated in a flat, dull voice.

"Why does it not surprise me?" Carl said. "All our lives people have been saying that he didn't look like either one of us. Ma'Dear cheated on Daddy, and, now, the truth finally comes out." He paced angrily over to the window.

"The two of you need to try to stay calm and take this in stride, now," Susan said. "Your brother is a sick man. He needs your support now."

Carl continued to stare out of the window. Junior sat

down slowly and put his face in his hands. Susan felt like a babysitter, but she was determined not to let either of them out of the room to confront their brother while things were so emotional. She sat down by Junior. None of them realized how much time had passed, but the light coming through the window showed the afternoon coming quickly to a close. They were startled by a voice.

"Mr. Durham?" A young woman stood in the doorway, both hands resting on a very pregnant belly. Jerome and Carl spun around.

"Lisa, is that you?" Jerome said. He stopped just short of embracing the young woman who had grown so close to their mother during her final illness and held out a hand to shake instead.

"Yes, it's me, one and the same," Lisa answered. "I mean, two and the same." She laughed, pointing at her belly.

"Congratulations," Carl said.

Junior smiled and nodded too. Lisa had been an attractive woman, and the baby weight swelling her face and belly did nothing to diminish her appeal. He thought she looked even more beautiful than ever. He chuckled to himself, remembering how Hattie had admonished him for admiring Lisa's looks. Lewis Durham, Jr., was a man who loved women, period.

"I heard about your brother being sick," Lisa said. "I came when I heard the news. They tell me that the councilman could die without a transfusion and that neither one of you is compatible."

"That's right," Carl and Junior said simultaneously.

"Listen, I think I can help you. Mrs. Durham was a

nice lady, and she confided quite a bit to me when she was here. She told me some things about herself I don't think she ever told anybody else," Lisa said.

"She told me about a man she used to know," continued Lisa, looking down at her hands, pausing briefly, then looking up again. "Mrs. Durham told me that he was her lover, and she had his baby – your brother, Jerome."

For a moment, there was silence. *Of course*, Susan thought. That's who Raymond was. It was why Hattie kept calling Jerome "Raymond" when she was in the grip of her dementia. Susan had suspected all along that Hattie had been tied up in some mysterious hanky panky at some point in her life, and the old woman had seemed to confirm it herself with her boast about having had three men. Now, Susan could do the math. Two of Hattie's infamous "men" had been her husbands, Lewis and Charlie, and the third was Jerome's father, Raymond Peace. Junior was first to break the silence.

"I'll be damned," he said.

"I knew it!" Carl jumped up, alarming Lisa. "That explains everything! Mama said she did it to protect us boys, but the reason she could do it so easy was because our daddy wasn't his daddy!"

Junior got to his feet. "Carl, what the hell are you talking about?" Junior shook his head, still trying to grasp Lisa's revelation, but it seemed like Carl was raving about something else.

"Jerome always was her favorite, and we always knew that, but I guess now we know why. Ma'Dear must have really loved this Raymond Peace guy to have his baby," Carl talked through it out loud.

"We don't know that," Junior said. He wanted to give Hattie the benefit of a doubt. "There might be some other things Mama didn't tell Lisa."

"Oh, she told Lisa quite enough," Carl snarled. "Just like she told me a few things when she didn't realize what she was saying."

"Carl, I'm asking you for the last time, what the hell you are talking about?" Junior said.

His brother didn't answer, but started to pace up and down, muttering to himself.

Susan tried to calm Carl down. He was getting worked up, ready to go berserk in his anger. Finally, some of the wind seemed to go out of him, and he sat down with his head in hands. Susan and Junior could see that Carl was at war with himself. His lips moved frantically while he shook his head and worked his hands. He finally looked up after a long time. He had made a decision.

"Junior, I got something to tell you," Carl began.

"Yes, brother?"

"I went to see Ma'Dear in the hospital one night when she was having a bad time of it," Carl continued. "She was having one of those spells when it seemed like she couldn't remember things right."

Junior nodded. He remembered well how confused Hattie used to get near the end. Sometimes, she didn't know whom she was talking to, where she was, or even what year it was. Talking to her had sometimes been a sad and often quite frustrating experience.

"Anyway, when I walked in that night, she thought I was daddy," Carl continued. He spoke with difficulty. "She started talking to me, calling me Lewis and everything, and saying she was sorry for what she did to me."

"What did she say she did?" Junior dreaded the answer.

Carl looked sad. "She told me she was sorry for smothering the life out of me the same night I was beat near to death by those white boys and too weak to keep her from doing it. Junior, do you hear what I'm saying, brother?"

Junior's eyes grew big. He sat down slowly. "Are you trying to tell me that Ma'Dear killed our father? That she ... smothered him?"

"And then went on to have her baby by another man," said Susan, giving in to the urge to spitefully chime in.

"Yes, Junior, I'm saying that our sweet little Ma'Dear was really just a deceitful, lying ..." Carl began but Junior stopped him.

"I won't hear you speaking ill of the dead," he told his brother quietly. His expression was menacing. "That's our mother you're talking about. We still got to show respect."

Carl sat down, muttering. As he sulked, it struck Junior just how much Carl really did resemble their father, especially when he had been in a similar mood, which had been often.

"Listen, I didn't come here to cause any hurt to this family," Lisa intervened. "I just wanted to help the councilman. I don't know if Raymond Peace is even still alive, but, if you can find out, maybe he can donate the bone marrow that his son needs."

"I'm sure that deep down we've all always known Mother Durham was not some kind of saint," Susan said. "And now we can be thankful for it because this lover of hers might be able to save your brother's life."

"And Jerome is still our brother, no matter who his daddy is," Junior added. He looked at Carl, and his tone was firm. "We still got the same blood, and we still had the same mother, God rest her soul. She can't answer to any of this now, dead in the ground, but we can still try to keep Rome from joining her too soon. Thank you for coming here, Lisa."

"You're welcome, Mr. Durham. And now I'll leave you be so that you all can figure out what you're going to do," said Lisa, getting up slowly. "Let me know if I can help. I'll be praying for this family."

She left the room with Susan right on her heels. Out in the hallway, Susan grabbed Lisa's elbow. The pregnant woman gently but firmly pulled her arm away and met the other woman's icy glare.

"Lisa, I appreciate what you've done for this family with this, shall we say, astonishing news," Susan said. "But now you need to mind your own business and stay away from Councilman Durham. He is a very sick man."

She stared hard at Lisa to make sure her words were sinking in. "He needs to devote all of his energy to fighting this illness, and he can't do that if he's doubting his beloved mother, worrying about his brothers, and wondering who his real father is. Jerome really doesn't need to hear about this right now."

"I know it's upsetting," Lisa said. "Believe me, I almost talked myself out of coming here today. But I just couldn't keep this to myself, knowing that the councilman's life was at stake."

Susan gave her a withering smile. "Upsetting is an

understatement, don't you think?" she said harshly. "I hope you realize you've turned this family upside down with your news. There was a good reason Mother Durham kept that information secret."

"If telling means the councilman's life might be saved, then I'm glad I did it, and you should be, too," Lisa retorted. "The elder Mrs. Durham would be too. I know how much that woman loved her son."

Before Susan could respond, Lisa had a horrifying thought. "You do mean to try to find his father, don't you?" she asked.

Susan gave her a chilly response. "Of course we are going to pursue every avenue to see that my husband gets well again, and this information certainly gives us a hopeful option," Susan said. "But I don't want to tell Jerome anything until we have something more definite to go on. For all we know, Raymond Peace might just have been another one of my mother-in-law's demented fantasies. So, if you don't mind, I'll ask you to stay away from my husband right now and kindly keep this news about his father to yourself. It would do nothing but cause a scandal if it gets out, anyway."

Lisa watched as Susan turned and walked away, designer heels clicking loudly on the tile. Lisa had initially admired Susan Durham, thinking her to be a lovely partner to her handsome husband. But the more she had observed Susan's interactions with the councilman's mother, the less she liked the ambitious, greedy woman. But Councilman Durham obviously treasured his wife and treated her like a china doll. *He's welcome to her*, Lisa thought. She was glad her business with the woman was done.

CHAPTER 11

At Jerome's request, Susan invited his brothers over. Junior agreed to come right away, but she ended up leaving a message for Carl with Trudy, who had no idea where her husband had gone off to. When Junior arrived, the eldest and youngest sons of Hattie Durham embraced for a long time.

"I'm sorry, bro'," Junior said awkwardly, sitting down in the chair next to the bed. He leaned over on his knees and clasped his hands between them.

"Lewis, what have you got to be sorry for?" Jerome asked.

"Just ... I thought for sure me or Carl would be able to donate what you need," Junior said. He looked miserable.

"We all did," Jerome said. He and his brother shared a bittersweet laugh.

"Where is that knucklehead Carl anyway?" Jerome asked. "I know we need to clear the air."

Junior shook his head. "Carl's gonna need some time. He's mad with Mama, Baby Brother, and he's mad at himself, just like I was for not being able to help you with this thing. But he'll come around. I'm gonna talk to him, too."

"Junior, what the hell was our mother thinking?" Jerome said.

"None of us have any way of knowing that, brother,"

Junior said. He scratched his head. "You know, back in those days, Ma'Dear used to have to go a long way to town alone to work. Who knows what kind of stuff she had to go through?"

Junior's gentle-hearted intelligence and loyalty to their mother was showing through. He was old enough to remember those hard times and compassionate enough to imagine what kind of things the young Hattie Durham might have faced back then.

Jerome was having trouble sorting out his emotions since learning that Lewis Durham was not his father. He supposed he had heard as many bad things as good ones about the man he had never known. He knew people sometimes tended to turn the dead into saints, understating the negative things about those people while overstating their best attributes. He and his brothers had heard a lot of praise about how hardworking and handsome the man had been, and, now, Jerome wondered how much of it was true.

He knew how hard their mother had worked to make sure the three boys grew up revering women. It had always been clear that she didn't want them to follow her first husband's example when it came to raising their hands in violence against females. With that upbringing, Jerome felt something was seriously wrong with anyone who would want to hit a woman. In that regard, it was actually a relief knowing his veins were clear of Durham's blood. And, yet, he carried the man's name, and the man's sons were his brothers. Jerome felt his confusion growing.

"Do you remember any other man coming around

before I was born, June?" Jerome said. He wasn't sure where to begin to find his real father, but it was increasingly urgent that he do so. Not just for my health, but for my sanity, he thought.

"I wouldn't know," Junior said. "I don't think so. Ma'Dear wouldn't have had some guy hanging around our house with Daddy there."

"I had to ask," Jerome said sheepishly. "I know it's a long shot, but maybe Aunt Doe or Aunt Pudge might know something."

Hattie's two cousins had been the closest people to her growing up. She'd spent most of her formative years in their home and considered them her sisters. Aunt Dorothea had been her best friend as well.

Junior was skeptical. "That's a long way back for those old ladies to remember."

"I know but I gotta try something," Jerome said. "Anyway, Aunt Doe is sharper than you and me both, put together," he laughed.

"It's gonna be a pain trying to explain all of this over the phone to those two, though," he continued, thinking it through. Both women were hard of hearing. "Maybe Susan and I can plan a trip down to the County to see if we can talk to them."

"Slow your roll, Baby Brother," said Junior, holding up his hands. "You just got out of the hospital, man. And you need serious treatment. I don't know what the doctor will say about you traveling right now. Maybe Donetta and I can go."

Junior saw it wasn't going to be easy to keep the news about Raymond Peace from Jerome for very long.

The man had also been fast thinking and determined, and being sick hadn't changed that.

"Lewis, I need to be the one to go," Jerome said. "It's my father we're trying to find out about."

"Let's just take this thing one step at a time. I'm going to check on Carl. Donetta and I are going to try to persuade Susan to have lunch with us. I'll stop by later," Junior said.

"Brother, if you can get that woman to eat a meal, I'll be forever indebted," Jerome said. He was joking but sincere. Susan looked like she had lost 10 pounds since this whole ordeal had started.

"Thank Donetta," Junior said. "That's all her, man. She loves working down there at your office, and she and Susan have gotten pretty close."

"Still, I know how you and Susan haven't been getting along lately," Jerome said. "Thank you for looking out for her."

"She's still family, man," Junior replied. "There's not a one of us who would let her starve looking out for you."

"I've asked Donetta to mind the office for a few days," Susan said. She knew she didn't have to worry; Donetta had proven to be extremely effective and had, somehow, managed to do it without ever raising her voice or repeating herself. People responded to Donetta's friendly charm much more readily than they ever did to Susan's brisk manner.

"I rented a car, and I'm going to pick it up tonight. I'm planning to leave first thing in the morning," she told Junior. She had asked both brothers if they wanted to go along for the trip. Carl was nowhere to be found, but Junior stepped up.

"I'm going with you."

"We're going to ask this man a huge favor and I want to make sure it's done in a way that will save everyone's dignity," she explained. Susan wasn't sure how Jerome's tall, hulking brother would come off to the Peace family. She wanted to handle the matter herself, and she told him so. But Junior stood firm.

"It's my brother we're going to ask the favor for," he justified. "And it's my mother who claims to have had this man's baby so that we even have to deal with him at all in the first place. I need to be there."

In the end, Susan relented. She hadn't been afraid to drive to Lowndes County alone, but it wasn't a bad idea to have her strong, tall brother-in-law as an escort either. She had been trying to come up with the words she would say to tell a stranger that her husband was the son he had never known about, and that son would maybe die without his help. Having Junior there might make it an easier story to sell; after all, Junior was Hattie's child too. Her legitimate child. Susan might have found the whole thing amusing if the circumstances weren't so dire.

She recalled the old woman talking about having done terrible things for love. Had getting pregnant with Jerome been one of those things?

Now, she and Junior sat in the old house with Hattie's favorite cousin, Dorothea. Aunt Doe had always been so proud of Jerome's success and his beautiful wife. Susan knew she would try hard to help. Once they sat down, Junior got right to the point.

"Did you and Mama know somebody named 'Raymond' when you all were growing up?"

Aunt Doe closed her eyes and wrinkled up in concentration. "No, I don't think so," she said slowly. "Not that I can recall. Young man, you know you meet so many people over the years, it gets hard to remember all of them."

"I know. What about Mama, though? Did she ever mention anybody to you, maybe a man?" Junior decided to try a different tactic. He shook his head and smiled, preparing to flatter her. "Sweet, sweet Aunt Doe. You are just like a second mother to us. Do you remember when Mama was working for those one ladies in town, and she used to leave us with you and Aunt Pudge a whole lot?"

"Yes, I remember that. Hattie was so proud of the

work she did at that job." Aunt Doe was beaming now, remembering a time that seemed to have been one of the happiest in her sister-friend's life. The girl had to hitch rides into town and, more often than not, stay several nights at a time. Her only worry was her boys, and, since she had her cousins for that, Hattie's job in town had been more of an escape and an adventure than a hardship. It had gotten her away from her sullen, drunken husband. It had given her a chance to meet new people and make new friends.

Aunt Doe's eyes popped wide open. "You know, now that I think of it, Hattie did say something about having a friend in town. She didn't want nobody to know about him, though." Aunt Doe looked around nervously.

"Do you know anything about him, Auntie? Maybe you know where we can find him," Susan asked.

"Well, now, cousin Hattie told me a lot of things, but she expected me to keep quiet about them," Aunt Doe said. "Lots of things. Even told me some things about you, girl."

"Things like what?" Susan was indignant and fearful at the same time; what secrets of hers had Mother Durham spilled?

But Aunt Doe only shook her head. "All that for another time. You all were asking me about Hattie's friend, and now I have some questions of my own. Why do you want to know?"

Susan and Junior exchanged concerned looks, but, finally, Susan nodded. Junior took that as the go-ahead to tell Aunt Doe about Jerome's illness.

"My, my, my, that poor baby," Aunt Doe crooned.

She was visibly upset at the news. She folded her arms and rocked from side to side, with tears welling up in her rheumy old eyes. She had a soft spot for Jerome, who had been the first infant she'd ever gotten to spend much time with besides her own baby sister. Hattie was a single mother by the time Jerome came along, relying on Aunt Doe and her sister to look after her kids while she struggled to find work and keep them all fed. So Aunt Doe and Aunt Pudge had seen Jerome through babyhood, and, as Junior had said earlier, Hattie's sons thought of the women as second mothers.

"Jerome is nobody's 'poor baby,'" Susan bristled. "Not if you tell us more about Hattie's friend. If he turns out to be Jerome's father, like we think, Jerome will be all right in no time." *Now, spill it, old lady*, Susan thought to herself.

Aunt Doe took her time, taking a sip of water, smacking her lips, and looking around again as if she expected Hattie herself to pop out of the walls.

"When Hoot would come back from town every week or so, she and I would sit up and sometimes have ourselves a drink or two," Aunt Doe said. "And she told me a secret about a man she got to know in town. She told me how she used to go down by the lumber yard and that the foreman there was so nice to her."

"Nice how?" Junior frowned.

"Oh, you know," Aunt Doe said. She lowered her voice to a whisper. "He would give her stuff, like candy and soda, or other things." The way she said "other things" left little doubt that the relationship between Hattie and this mystery man had probably been intimate.

"Was his name Raymond Peace?" Susan jumped in

impatiently. "We need to know how to find him."

"Raymond," Aunt Doe exclaimed. She laid her finger along the side of her nose, trying to remember. "Seems like the name was something like that. Raymond Peace."

Junior and Susan exchanged glances. The address they had gotten from the database for Raymond Peace was close to the Lowndes County Line, and Junior knew the Southern Lumber Company was down that way as well. Any fool could easily fill in the blanks between the story Lisa had given them about Raymond Peace and the information Aunt Doe was hesitantly sharing now.

"And now that you mention it, Hattie wanted to name that boy Raymond, but I told her she better not," Doe continued. She looked around as if afraid someone else was listening. "I told that girl it would be nothing but trouble if she named that boy anything else but some kind of family name, because he didn't favor anybody in the family. Not anybody we knew, anyway."

"Aunt Dorothea, it's been good seeing you, but we've got to go now," Susan said.

"Oh, no, won't you all stay and have some dinner? We haven't seen you in so long," Aunt Doe pouted.

Even though Susan saw that Junior was inclined to say "yes," she shook her head rapidly.

"The sooner we get this done, the better," Susan said. "I don't want to waste any time finding out if this man is going to be able to help Jerome."

"Oh, yes, child, Baby Brother needs all the help he can get now, have mercy," Aunt Doe said.

Susan winced at the nickname Aunt Doe called Jerome. Aunt Doe didn't notice. She wiped at her eyes with a handkerchief as she saw them to the door, sending them off with hugs and kisses to pass on to Jerome, Carl, and the others.

Susan and Junior were ready to be on their way. It was time to find Raymond Peace.

❧ CHAPTER 13 ❧

The first thing that came to Junior's mind when the woman answered the door was that she looked familiar. She was fairly tall and somewhat heavyset, with reddish-colored dark hair, tan skin, and dimples. A copper-colored braid threaded with silver hair was wound into a bun at the back of her neck.

I know her, Junior thought.

"Can I help you?" the woman asked.

Susan and Junior spoke at the same time. "Yes, we're looking for Raymond Peace?"

Recognition then dawned on Junior as he looked at the bespectacled woman. "Tina? Albertina Peace?" he asked.

Albertina peered at Junior over the rims of her glasses. "Lewis Durham?"

"Yes, yes, that's me." Junior allowed himself to be pulled into an embrace against the big bosom that he had admired as a young man. Peace. He didn't know how he had not made the connection sooner. Now, he wracked his brains, trying to figure out the timing. Just when exactly had his mother had her affair with Raymond Peace? Their father had been long dead and Jerome was almost a teenager when she and Albertina worked together at the school.

Susan was staring with a puzzled expression on

her face. "You two know each other?" She said.

"Oh, yes. His mother and I used to work together many years ago. And how is your mother?" Albertina asked.

"She passed a few years ago," Junior replied.

"Oh, may the good Lord rest her soul. I'm sorry to hear that," said Albertina, looking at him and Susan. "I know what it is to lose a parent."

Before Albertina could answer, Susan butted in impatiently.

"That's not why we're here," she said.

"Tina, this is a crazy coincidence," Junior said. "We're here concerning my brother Jerome," Junior added.

"Jerome?" Albertina's brow wrinkled as she recalled what she knew of Hattie Durham's family." I don't believe I ever got to meet Jerome. I think he was sick the entire time I was working with Hattie," she said.

Junior nodded. It was an effort to recall events from so many years ago.

"I remember her talking about him all the time, though," Albertina said. "She would go on and on about her baby Jerome."

"That baby you remember is now my husband," Susan interjected. She was over the small talk. "And he's a very sick man right now."

Jerome frowned at her, then turned back to Albertina. "May we come in?"

"Of course, forgive me," said Albertina, sweeping the door wide open. "I did not mean to be rude. It's a surprise to see Hattie Durham's son on my front porch after all these years."

It was a surprise indeed. Albertina had never understood why Hattie Durham had not been particularly nice to her during the brief time they'd worked together at an elementary school up in Montgomery. In the end, Hattie had stopped a nasty old man from forcing himself on Albertina, who had never gotten over the humiliation. The independent young teacher had come home after the fright and made herself content to live with her parents ever since. Albertina had only met Junior once or twice, and he had been a polite young man. Though he made her a little nervous, she was pleased to see him now, still tall and looking good.

"We're here to see Raymond Peace," Susan persisted.

Albertina frowned, confused. "My brother's not in just now."

"Raymond Peace is your brother?" Susan was incredulous.

"Yes, but he's not here right now. Unless you mean my father ..." said Albertina, her voice trailing off as she turned to look out the window. "Oh wait, I think that's him pulling up in the driveway. "

Albertina had never gotten over her shyness around men, and Junior's masculine presence was a bit much for her now. She was so relieved at her brother's return home that she practically skipped to greet him at the door, an awkward behavior for a woman of her age.

Susan had been checking out the Peace's living room. The decor was a bit old fashioned for her taste, and she wondered about the brother and sister who were living in the same house at their age, but it didn't matter.

In the meantime, Junior observed Albertina carefully.

He was a man who appreciated women and never had trouble finding something beautiful about every female he met. Albertina Peace was no exception. She seemed to be a gentle and intelligent woman who had somehow never outgrown certain girlish ways. It was clear that she had never gotten married or had children of her own, and Junior thought it was a shame. He had no doubt she would have made a fine wife and mother.

The man who got out of the car came up the walk and into the house, and Susan and Lewis, Jr., were both dumbstruck. The man that stood before them looked exactly like Jerome. He was greeted enthusiastically by Albertina, who rushed back up the walk behind him. He smiled and nodded, and shook both Jerome and Susan's hands as Albertina made hasty introductions.

Raymond Peace, Jr., invited them to sit, and Albertina rushed to bring refreshments for everyone.

"Appreciate your hospitality, Mr. Peace," Junior said.

"You can call me RJ. Now, what brings you here? Other than your mother working with my sister in Montgomery?" Though his sister had never said a word about it, as the closest person to her, Raymond had known something bad had happened to Albertina there. He had kept her under his protective wing ever since. He kept a cool smile on his face, wondering what these people could possibly want with his family now. The woman, Susan, locked her piercing grey gaze on RJ.

"Look, Mr. Peace," she began. Susan hated nicknames. "We don't have time to waste and there's no easy way to tell you this."

She pulled out her wallet and showed him a photo.

She let him look at it for a minute before saying anything else. Raymond Peace looked up slowly, meeting Susan's eyes with a questioning look of his own.

"That man is my husband. His obvious resemblance to you is because you have the same father," Susan said.

Albertina's hands went to her face. Before RJ could speak, Susan went on.

"My husband, Jerome, is ill, Mr. Peace, and gravely so. We came here to find his father and to ask if he would consider contributing his bone marrow to Jerome. He can save my husband's life."

Albertina looked even further stricken. "I'm sorry, I didn't get to tell them," she said. RJ patted his sister's hand.

"Our father passed away last year," he said.

"God rest his soul," Albertina added fervently.

The others in the room followed her gaze to the mantelpiece, where a framed photograph of their family stood. It had been taken years ago, when RJ was a long-legged teenager, the year before Albertina had gone to teach in Montgomery. Their father, Raymond Peace, stood tall and proud over his beaming family. His expression was serious, but laughter lurked just beneath the depths of his dark gold eyes. Just like RJ's. Just like Jerome's.

"Our condolences to you both," Junior said.

"That's what I meant when I said I know what it is to lose a parent," Albertina said. "We all miss daddy. Mama, the most."

Susan Chalfont Durham had always been focused when she wanted something, and hearing of Raymond

Peace's death did not forestall her persistence now.

"Of course, we are so sorry for your loss," she said. "You must let us know if there is anything we can do to help you. But, Mr. Peace – RJ – you are Jerome's brother. Maybe there's something you can do to help us. That is, if you're willing."

"Susan!" Junior whispered. To his mind, this was a touchy situation that required delicate handling. He could not believe Susan was being so blunt. But then again, Jerome's wife had always been a pistol. She wasn't one to beat around the bush when she was on a mission.

"You might be a compatible donor for him as well. Would you be willing to be tested, at least?" Susan pressed.

RJ stood up. "I'm sorry. This is a lot to take in all at once. I'm going to ask you to leave now."

Still a bit overexcited, Albertina shook her head. "RJ, don't be so rude to our guests. Don't listen to him now," she said to Susan and Junior. Susan panicked

"Mr. Peace, please, I didn't mean to be so presumptuous," she said. "But my husband does not have a lot of time to waste. I know this is difficult information to digest all of a sudden, but there is time for that later."

RJ frowned down at her in a look that reminded her so much of Jerome that she choked back a sob. He opened the door and gestured wide.

"We're staying at the Hampton in town," said Junior, stepping in between Susan and RJ, and putting his hand out to shake. "We'll be there for a couple of days if you want to get in touch later. It's good to see you again, Albertina," Junior said with a cordial nod. He grabbed

Susan by the elbow, and pushed her forward and out.

"He'll do the right thing, won't he?" Susan was in shock. "RJ will want to help Jerome."

Junior felt sympathy for RJ and Albertina. But then again, every family had a tomcat or two in it; hell, Junior was one himself. He felt a little guilty, imagining what it was like for those two to hear that their daddy was one. He had always heard that his own daddy was one and that his granddaddy Benton was one too. Jerome was glad his twins Lashonna and Latasha already knew his other kids. Donetta had insisted on it.

"The man needs time to think about it," Junior said. Though he was annoyed, his voice was firm but gentle. "And we're gonna give him all the time he needs."

CHAPTER 14

S usan had regained her composure by the time they got back to the hotel. She turned down Junior's invitation to join him for dinner. She suspected he was just being polite anyway. He was just as shook up by meeting the Peace siblings as she had been. They both needed time to process what had happened.

Restless, Susan took a taxi to the mall. She wanted to look for some much-needed new accessories for her campaign wardrobe: a few scarves, a handbag, maybe some new shoes. Shopping always made her feel better. She was rushing from out of a store when she dropped her keys. She bent to pick them up, and, as she stood, Susan looked up into the familiar face of Eleanor Foster, Chancelly Foster's sister. Susan fought back the panicked nausea that held her frozen in place. Eleanor Foster's face twisted in disgust. "You!" said Eleanor, making no effort to disguise her distaste.

"Eleanor Foster, it is certainly a surprise to see you again," said Susan, mustering up her most polite-sounding voice.

"Surprise, indeed," Eleanor said through clenched teeth. "It's Eleanor Foster-Lancet now. I certainly had hoped you had gone far, far away from here and crawled back under whatever dark southern rock you originally crawled out from, Susan Chalfont."

"It's Susan Durham now," said Susan, mimicking the other woman's snotty tone, but it was lost on Eleanor, who continued.

"Yes, I do recall hearing or seeing somewhere about you getting married. To a black politician," Eleanor said. "My, my, our poor Chancelly must be turning in his grave right now. To think, a brother of mine ever thought of marrying you," she said, making *tsk-tsking* sounds.

"Please, Eleanor, don't do this in public," Susan said. She was just a tone shy of begging, and she hated herself for it. But it was better than having Eleanor Foster-Lancet cause a scene in public. The last thing Jerome's campaign needed was the news that his wife was involved in a catfight in the mall.

"I would have thought a lady of fine breeding such as yourself would wish me well and let bygones be bygones," Susan hissed under her breath. She couldn't believe the woman's nerve.

"What I wish is that your poor husband eventually finds out what a piece of work you really are, Susan Chalfont, and, if I ever meet him, I will advise him to divorce you immediately and run screaming the other way," said Eleanor, who turned her nose up, proud of her cutting words.

With Susan fixed in place, Eleanor could not resist adding further insult. "If ever there was any good to be had from Chancelly's death, I'd say it's that he escaped your filthy clutches." She looked around with a superior smile on her face, tapping her hands with her gloves.

"Amazing, isn't it," Eleanor continued, talking into the air. "What one man knows will taint his race, another man is sure will elevate his. But I guess the trick is in knowing what's what, isn't it? I wonder if there are a few things your poor husband ought to know about you."

Susan recognized a threat when she heard one. Her eyes narrowed. "I had hoped we could remain polite, but I promise you this, Eleanor: If you ever try to drag me down, you can be sure I will drag you right down with me."

Eleanor snorted. Susan had been so caught up in her exchange with Eleanor that she hadn't noticed the man accompanying her old enemy. A few fine silver threads ran through his perfectly cut, champagne-pale hair. He was solid and muscular in a finely cut crème-colored suit with a blue silk tie that exactly matched his eyes. Now, he spoke sharply.

"Mother, your manners!" He looked around to see who might be watching, then turned a dazzling smile on Susan. "Miss, if you please, allow me to apologize for my mother. It's been a trying day, and she can be rude when her temper is running short." He gave a short polite bow. Susan nodded in return.

"Craig, you do not presume to speak for me," Eleanor sniffed.

"Then surely you can be more civil than this," he said. "Introduce us, please."

"I will not," Eleanor jerked her arm from her son's grip.

Craig looked around again, and smiled again at Susan. He seemed embarrassed.

"All right, then, I will introduce myself," he said. "I am Craig Lancet. It appears you already know my mother."

"And I'm Susan Chalfont Durham. Clearly, I knew your mother long ago."

"You did not know me. You were merely acquainted with my brother," Eleanor retorted. "My dead brother, Chancelly," she added pointedly.

"Pleasure to meet you, Mrs. Durham ... or, it would be, under different circumstances, I'm sure." The blond man leaned forward to shake Susan's hand.

"Craig, we must be going now," Eleanor said. Without another word, she turned on her heel and huffed away. Craig threw Susan a final embarrassed smile and ran after her.

Susan buried her face in her hands. When she was sure they were gone, she sank down into a nearby chair, her chest heaving with relief.

Eleanor Foster. After all those years, she was the last person Susan wanted to see. She had wanted to bury those memories along with Chance Foster. Instead, here she was, trembling with humiliation just as she had so many times in the past under the scrutiny of Chance's sister.

Susan heaved a sigh, trying to compose herself. She wanted to scream. This whole thing, she thought, was Hattie Durham's fault. She and Junior had come here, chasing down his mother's lies and deceptions, and the chase had driven Susan right into the arms of a past she wanted to forget. But when she closed her eyes, the memories played like a movie on the screen of her mind. Chance had taken her up to the water tower that night, looking more serious than he ever had in the past. Once they got there, instead of kissing her and lifting her dress like she'd expected him to, Chance had held her hands firmly and looked into her eyes.

"Look, Susan, you've never told me much about your past, and I haven't asked," he began. "But I do need to know something."

"Anything, Chance," Susan had said in her best honey-sweet drawl. Chance usually found her Southern Belle act irresistible.

"I've got to know you aren't going to embarrass me once we get married," he said. He was serious. "My family is important in this town. Did you know that ours is one of the oldest families in this county? My father's patients are among the wealthiest, most influential names you can find for miles around, and I cannot bring shame of any kind to the Foster name. Do you hear what I'm saying, Susan?"

"I hear you, Chance. You're hurting me," said Susan, trying to pull her arm away.

"No, I'm not sure you do hear me, Susan," Chance said. He held her even tighter. "So, let me make it clear. I cannot marry you and then one day have a little dark child appear in our family cradle. I cannot have that happen. Do you understand?"

Susan's eyes were large and frightened as she nodded. This was not like Chance. His sister Eleanor had put those words in his mouth. Susan was sure of it. Eleanor and her friends had been going out of their way to corner her as often as possible, making snide comments and rude remarks. Purposely asking provocative questions about her unusual last name and tan skin.

Eleanor didn't know anything for sure, but her

instincts were dead-on when it came to her suspicions about her brother's girlfriend. While it had been entertaining to harass the girl, the family inheritance was a deadly serious matter that could only have one outcome. Susan Chalfont was no more than a mutt whose dark blood would not be allowed to taint the pure Foster gene pool. The girl had to go.

It was clear that Eleanor had gotten to her brother and whispered her effective poison in his ear. It didn't matter if he loved Susan or not. Tears welled up in Susan's eyes as Chance slowly released his grip on her. His own sky blue eyes were cold as ice.

"So," he continued, without breaking his gaze, "if there's any chance that might happen, any at all, then we're just going to put it to an end right here. Right now."

Susan didn't blink. "I want to respect you, Susan," Chance continued. "If there's a chance at all this thing I just described to you could happen, I want you to give the ring back. Nothing more has to be said. Give my ring back, and I'll walk away."

Susan stared at him for a moment. This was Chance Foster, the man who was supposed to be her future husband. There was absolutely no compassion in eyes at all, just a hard, cold expectation. Susan took off the ring and placed it in his palm. She imagined she saw a flicker of hurt in his face as he turned his back on her. No matter now. Susan put her hands up to his chest and pushed as hard as she could.

"Ma'am?" Susan startled, but she recognized the voice without turning around. If she had not just met the man, she would have thought a ghost was speaking to her; Chance Foster's ghost. His nephew looked and sounded just like Chance would have, had he lived to be that age. Susan gathered her wits before turning to face the man with a dazzling smile.

"I'm sorry to bother you again," Craig Lancet said. "I just wanted to apologize for my mother back there."

"Oh, really, there's no need." Susan tried to laugh it off. She realized she was shaking and grabbed at the back of a chair for support.

Craig Lancet smiled. "May we sit for a moment? Here, let me get that for you." He pulled the chair out and, gently guiding her elbow, helped her to sit. Susan caught a whiff of his cologne. It was subtle and expensive.

"Listen, I don't know what was going on back there between the two of you and I certainly don't mean to pry," Craig said. "But let's be frank. I know what a harridan my mother can be when she sets her mind to it or she decides she doesn't like someone. I could see that she was giving you hell back there, even though you were trying to be polite."

Susan shook her head and smiled. Why couldn't she pull herself together? Craig's smile was dazzling. He really was quite a handsome young man. It struck her again how much Craig resembled his uncle, Chance, the uncle he had never met. Though it had been years ago – decades ago – Susan remembered that Chance had, at one time, made her feel the exact same way.

"It seems that Eleanor has never forgotten our differences of long ago," she said breezily. "Some people are just that way. But please don't trouble yourself, Mr. Lancet. I bear her no grudge."

"She could certainly learn something from you," Craig replied. "It seems like my mother and all of her close friends are like a bunch of mean old cats who spend their time spitting and scratching, always looking for the next hair to fall out of place or a new bone to pick."

He rolled his tongue around his mouth in a boyish motion. "Anyway, I wanted to give you my business card," he said. "Not that you'd ever have cause to contact me, but I want you to know that I believe in letting bygones be bygones. If there's ever anything I can do for you, please let me know. Perhaps there might be even something I can do to help your husband's campaign. Maybe between the two of us there is some way we could bury whatever old hatchet that's kept our families apart."

Susan had the feeling Craig's words had a double meaning as he looked directly into her eyes. Had she been a younger woman, she would have blushed. But now, she held his gaze with confidence. Craig chuckled.

"Beautiful women like you are always so serene. I wish my mother could display that kind of grace," he said.

Susan was struck silent. Had she heard him correctly? This good-looking young man thought she was beautiful. Her husband used to tell her that every day. Jerome used to shower her with compliments, saying her hair looked like it had been kissed by the sun or that her eyes looked like grey jewels. Looking at Craig now, Susan was reminded of how she used to react when Jerome would tell her he'd never dated a girl with such light skin. He would make a naughty comment, like asking her if she'd like some coffee with her cream, and she'd giggle and welcome him into her arms. But then insecurities would creep in and Susan would get serious.

"Is that why you want me, Jerome? Because of my light skin? That's what all the other girls think, anyway," she had asked him on several different occasions. Though their snobbery hurt, Susan took a lot of satisfaction in knowing jealousy is what drove the other girls' meanness. Each and every one of them would have killed to be dating her fine-as-hell Jerome Durham.

When she'd say something like that, Jerome would frown. His golden eyes would get hazy and thoughtful. Finally, he'd take her chin in his hand and look into her eyes.

"The reason I want you has nothing to do with your looks, Miss Susan, or your skin color, even if you happen to be the most beautiful girl I know. But all that pretty is just a bonus. The reason I want you so much, the reason I love you so much, is because you happen to be just right for me." He'd nick her chin and kiss her. "Believe that."

Yes, those had been happier days for the couple. What Susan hadn't told Jerome was that the reason she accused him of being color-struck was that her pale skin was at the center of her own troubles. It was the reason why she'd agreed to go with him in the first place and why, ultimately, she'd agreed to marry him. She was still licking her wounds after being rejected by Chancelly Foster. Susan had wanted so badly to marry that boy and be accepted into the rich, white world he inhabited, but, after his death, she'd had to convince herself that it wasn't what she had wanted at all. After all, as the wife of a wealthy white doctor, which Chance would have become had he lived, she would have lived on pins and needles, constantly worried that someone might find out who she really was. And who was she, really?

It occurred to Susan that she didn't even really have any definitive knowledge of her own ethnicity. She didn't have a strong enough recollection of her own mother to even be able to guess what race the woman belonged to. Susan had always assumed her father, Oscar, was white, with his dirty blond hair, expensive clothes and the refined way that he spoke. But she had also inferred that she was of mixed parentage from her experiences growing up, including the circumstances surrounding Baby Joe's coming to live at Minerva's. Why would the baby boy's family threaten to drown the infant simply for existing? There was also the willingness of the Burns' family to welcome her into their home. They wouldn't have brought home a white girl, would they? And even if they were – and although she couldn't be entirely sure – Susan was fairly certain that Minerva wouldn't have sent a little white girl to live with a black family. It all seemed to suggest that there was black blood running through her veins and that at least some of it was contributed by the white-looking Oscar Chalfont. But there was just no sure way to know.

As an adult, Susan realized that she could have tried to find out more. Her birth certificate read, "Baby girl Roker. Mother: Melissa Roker. Father: Unknown." Susan had never tried to find her mother's family, preferring not to know anything more about them than the document revealed. Susan had decided she could still use that uncertainty to her advantage.

As the wife of Chance Foster, Susan would have

tenuously become a member of carefree white society, but she would always stand apart from the other women in the group. They would have no doubts about the fact that they truly belonged while her identity would always be in question. On the other hand, she didn't have to worry about being accepted by Jerome's community. The people there were just as color-struck as anyone else and could be counted on to welcome and even up to her as the pretty, light-skinned wife of her successful, black husband. As Mrs. Jerome Durham, she could feel superior to all the other women who wished they were in her shoes. The decision to marry Jerome so soon after Chance's death had not been a difficult one to make.

Susan was still determined to live out the myth that she had created. Instead of calling herself by the adoptive last name of Burns, she used that of her biological father, Oscar Chalfont. That way no one could trace her back to the black couple who had taken her in. If anyone asked, she'd tell them her parents were the late Oscar and Lissie Chalfont of Shreveport, Louisiana, which should keep anyone from trying to trace her that way, too.

Other than the birthday and Christmas cards she regularly sent, Susan herself rarely reached out to her adoptive parents. Henrietta Burns had gone to her death heartbroken over her adopted daughter's polite and chilly attitude. As a man, Woodrow Burns thought he better understood Susan's need to make her own way, and he did what he could to make it easier for her. He left her several pieces of property outright as well as providing generously for her in his will. He never demanded the demonstrations of affection from the girl that his wife seemed to crave, and, for that, Susan was especially grateful.

Though she lived on the allowance provided for her through her inheritance from Woodrow Burns, Susan allowed people to believe that her late biological father, Oscar Chalfont, had left her a modest fortune that allowed her to go to school and live independently. Susan Chalfont was a woman of her own making.

Her cream-colored skin and the mystery surrounding her origins made her that much more desirable to Jerome Durham, who sensed in her the need for the affection of a strong man. His mistake was in underestimating her even stronger need for power, to be the center of attention, and to manipulate everything according to the order she desired. The pretty girl hadn't grown up exactly fatherless, but she had been deprived of a stable male authority figure for much of her life. By the time Woodrow Burns came along, she was already a teenager, hardened by a difficult life and fairly resistant to any overt attempts to try to control her. She longed to live her life on her own terms, free from the constraints people would have put on her based on things beyond her control.

Susan Chalfont had made herself into a formidable woman. She was no longer just another one of "that no-good Oscar's little orphan bastards" as she, Joe, and Daisy had often been called. By giving her his name, Jerome had put her right in the position she wanted to be in – as a beautiful, powerful woman about to become the wife of the most powerful man in their city.

The future first lady of Sharon, Alabama, reached out

for Craig Lancet's card. He grabbed her hand and held it for a moment, challenging her with his eyes. His message was clear: he did find her attractive. Susan fought to keep her composure as he stroked her palm with his middle finger. The invitation was unmistakable. But Susan Chalfont Durham was a lady, if nothing else. She drew her hand free.

"Goodbye, Craig," she said. Her southern accent had never seemed more pronounced. She suspected he found it attractive. "If I find that I ever do need anything, I will certainly give you a call."

The next morning dragged on in silence at the hotel without a call from RJ Peace. Susan wanted to call him, but Junior firmly forbade her to do so. "The ball is in his court now," he said, carrying their bags to check out. "If he decides to call, he will do so. We don't have to be in town for him to reach us."

Susan was incensed as she took the wheel and got on the highway back to Sharon. Junior kept telling her to slow down, but she was distracted by her thoughts and kept speeding up. Finally, a state trooper pulled them over, infuriating her even more. She practically tore the citation out of the officer's hand and glared at his retreating back in the rearview mirror. Junior suggested that they pull in for coffee at the next stop to give her time to calm down. As they sat down, Susan's hands kept flying to her lips. She had chewed her nails ragged.

"You sure are making a big deal out of a little traffic ticket," Junior observed. "I hate to think how you're going to act if they charge you with Ma'Dear's murder."

Susan nearly spit out her coffee. "Excuse me?" she said.

"You heard me," Junior said. He watched her calmly. "What would you do if they came to you and said you were being formally charged with murdering my mother? Your own husband's mother." Susan shook her head and rolled her eyes impatiently.

"Why on earth would they ever do that? Now?" Susan was incredulous. "Lewis, the matter was settled years ago. The hospital and the police investigated what happened to Mother Durham, and they determined it to be an accident. Officially. A tragedy, yes, but an accident."

"Oh, yes, that's right, an accident," Junior said sarcastically. His expression did not change. "I forgot, that's what they call breathing machines that unplug themselves and sick old women who slam their heads on the floor just to give hospital personnel something to do: Accidents."

"Junior, please," Susan said. She did not normally use his nickname, finding it ludicrous to call a grown man by such a childish name, but, under the circumstances, the name seemed to fit. Under the table, Susan clasped and wrung her hands, but tried to maintain a cool expression for Junior's benefit.

"Mother Durham's death was hard on all of us," she said. "I know that more than anyone. I'm married to her favorite son, remember?"

"Jerome even feels responsible for what happened to her," Susan went on. "Still. You know he regrets so many of the decisions we made regarding her care, but he's finally getting over it and moving on with his life. Why don't you try to do the same?"

"Baby Brother moved on long ago, as far as I can tell," Junior said bitterly. "He didn't skip a beat, did he, winning that city council election, and, now, he's gotten to be so full of himself that he thinks he can run the whole town."

"Oh, Junior," Susan sighed. She ran tired hands through her hair. "Winning that election was probably the only thing that kept your brother going after Mother Durham died. I think Jerome won that city council seat mainly because of her death, not in spite of it. He wanted her to be proud of him."

"She was," Junior said. His tone was flat.

"That's right. And he's going to make a magnificent mayor, too, and I'd like to know he can count on having his brother's support."

"He does," Junior replied in the same monotone voice.

"Well, then," Susan said. She sat back and stirred her coffee. "I don't know how you can accuse me of even thinking of harming your mother, knowing how close she and Jerome were. But if you really want to support Jerome, you won't mention this again." She sipped her coffee and looked around for the waitress, as the cup had grown cold.

"Look, Lewis, your mother and I may not have been the best of friends, but I respected her. I did my best to get along with her, and I took care of her because I love Jerome." Susan sat back, thinking that was the end of it, but Junior leaned forward.

"You took care of her, all right," he snarled. "You wanted her out of the picture so that you and Jerome could be the perfect couple living high on the hog: rich, free and without a care in the world ... and without his old mother to worry about."

"That's not true," Susan said. She was shaking. "And anyway, Lewis," she leaned forward, on the defensive now, "however your mother died, it was a mercy, don't you think? Just like she thought what she did to your father was a mercy."

Junior slammed his hands down on the table, restraining himself from striking her. Watching him, Susan eased back slowly, with a grim, triumphant smile on her face.

"Your mother was an old, sick woman, and she was losing her mind, besides," she said. "Who even knows how many years she had left?"

When he didn't say anything, she continued. "She hated being in the hospital, and she probably would have stroked out or had a heart attack on the spot if she had woken up to find herself in my house," she said cruelly. "I did the old bird a favor," she muttered under her breath. But Junior heard her. He leaned forward again.

"You did what?" he said menacingly.

"Nothing," Susan said quickly. She saw that Junior was on the edge of his self control, and she did not wish to provoke him any further. "All I said was that we did her a favor – Jerome and I – by taking care of her when nobody else could, even if she would have hated knowing I was involved at all."

"Don't think I didn't hear what you said. Don't you ever call my mother out of her name again," Junior said. He glared at her.

Thinking he was placated, Susan reached out and touched his hand.

"Lewis, we have to put this thing behind us. We came here together because we want to save Jerome, remember?" she cajoled. "That's what Mother Durham would have wanted, isn't it? For Jerome to be okay. That's not going to happen if the people he's depending on now are fighting over a crazy misunderstanding. And an old one at that."

She watched him carefully, amazed that he did not pull his hand away.

"And that's all this is. A misunderstanding," she said.

"Oh, is that what you call it?" Junior did pull his hand away now, slowly.

"Yes. Yes, I do, because you've got it all wrong," Susan said. "I know you're still hurt over your mother's death, and you're looking for somebody to blame. But the truth is, Mother Durham lived a long life and her body and her mind were finally beginning to fail her. We should all just be thankful that she passed peacefully."

She looked at him. "Maybe it's hard for you to let go because you haven't really lost anyone who was close to you before," she spoke again, but it was the wrong thing to say. Junior slammed the table again.

"I lost my daddy," he said.

Susan was quick to respond. "That's right, and unlike me – because I'm innocent – your mother admitted to killing that man. I'm sorry to say it, but did you ever think maybe she got what she had coming? Maybe her dying had nothing to do with me, or with you or your brothers, but maybe some divine purpose was at work, and it was time for her to answer in some way to her own crimes. I know you don't like hearing this, Lewis, but maybe you should think about that."

When Junior finally spoke, it was a low growl between his teeth. "I swear on my Ma'Dear's grave, I don't know what Jerome sees in you," he said. He backed away from the table slowly, then turned and left the dining room.

Shaken, Susan leaned back against the booth and tried to compose herself. She gestured to a waitress, who came and freshened her coffee. Susan had a sip and then pulled a compact from her purse. She smoothed her hair and studied herself in the mirror, willing a calm expression to come and smooth out the fine lines and wrinkles that frowning etched into her pale complexion. Lewis, Jr., might be angry now but he needed to get over it because it was a long drive back home and one they had to make alone together.

She didn't know what she was going to do about him, but she knew one thing: she had to do something.

CHAPTER 16

"Jerome, I spoke to Reverend Solomon on your behalf," Trudy Durham said. "I hope you don't mind." She was more dressed up than usual for work and carried a box of dark chocolates for her favorite brother-in-law, whom she had stopped by to see on her way in to work that day. Trudy had wanted Carl to come with her, but he was not in bed when she got up that morning.

Jerome beamed at his sweet little sister-in-law, letting his smile speak for him. Of course he didn't mind. Rodney Solomon had been one of his best friends as a boy and had grown up to be a church leader, as everyone had known he would.

Rodney strode forward with an extended hand, and the men pulled each other into a warm embrace.

"Pastor Solomon," Jerome said gravely.

"Brother Jerome," the pastor returned. The two old friends look solemnly at one another. The compassion Jerome saw in the reverend's eyes made him feel instantly calm.

"I brought along some of the other brothers, and we would like to pray with you, Jerome."

Jerome nodded, and Reverend Solomon went to the door and opened it. Six men filed in, each greeting Jerome warmly and solemnly, then Reverend Solomon, standing at the head of the bed, addressed the room.

"The Lord said, 'Seek,'" Reverend Solomon called.

"And you shall find," the other preachers responded.

"And then the Lord said 'knock!'" Reverend Solomon roared.

"And the door shall be opened," responded the others.

"Ask a favor!" intoned the reverend.

"And it shall be done," the others said. A chorus of "amens" and "have mercys" followed.

"And so this day we will follow the Word," said Reverend Solomon, bowing his head to pray. The others did so as well. Jerome closed his eyes and clasped his hands too.

"We seek, O Lord, a healing today for our Brother Jerome here. Your humble servant, who has devoted his very life to the betterment of this community, in his own way tending to your flock. Heed us now in his time of need," the reverend prayed. "Hear us knock upon your door, Lord. None other has the power."

"The favor that we ask is that you put your loving arms around this family and lend them strength in this time of doubt. Our bodies are weak but we know all things are possible with you. Touch this man, Lord. As we gather in prayer around our Brother Jerome, we ask that he will feel your touch through our humble hands. The grace is thine, and thine alone." The others murmured in agreement and supplication.

Jerome trembled as Reverend Solomon placed his palms on Jerome's forehead. The reverend nodded to the others, and they reached out to place their palms on his arms, his cheek, and anywhere his bare skin allowed.

Outside the door, Trudy crossed herself. "Have mercy," she whispered. She looked up at Susan, who was pacing back and forth.

"Your doubt won't help Jerome," Trudy said gently. "You've got to have faith."

"I know you all mean well, but I honestly don't see how all of this is going to help him," Susan snapped. "If anything, having all of these people around and all of this commotion will probably just wear him out worse than before. He needs to conserve his strength."

"Jerome believes," Trudy said gravely.

"Jerome is just going along with this because you told him it would have pleased Hattie," Susan said. "Otherwise, he wouldn't have time for this."

"Mother Durham raised her sons in the church. All three of them," Trudy persisted.

"That's true, and look at what good it did Carl," Susan snapped. "Oh, and I notice he's not here and neither is Lewis, Jr. That tells you what they think of it."

"Well, you know I hope both of those men find their way back to some kind of redemption in the Lord's own time," Trudy said. "But, right now, it's Jerome that needs our support, our love, our prayers ... all that he can get." She looked Susan carefully in the eye. "Especially yours."

"Oh, Trudy, of course I am praying for my husband to get well," Susan buried her face in her hands with frustration. "But we have to do something. I mean, we just can't sit around waiting for a miracle."

At that moment, a nurse rushed up to Susan. "Dr. Mathieson would like to see you and your husband right away."

"I think they might be finished in there," Trudy said. There was a mad scramble as the women entered Jerome's hospital room. The men had finished praying and were talking about sports. Reverend Solomon shook Jerome's hand and promised to return later in the week. As he joined the line of men filing out of the room past Susan, the reverend stopped to press his hands in hers and kiss her cheek.

"Have faith, sister," he said. Susan nodded. As soon as he left, she rushed to Jerome's side.

"Dr. Mathieson is on his way. He wants to talk to us," she said. As she straightened his pillows, she looked in his eyes. "That is, if you're up to it after all of that excitement. Even in the hospital, you know how to draw a crowd."

Jerome laughed. "That visit did me a world of good," he said. "It was great to see Rodney and those guys. It's been too long."

Susan started to sit down, but, just then, her phone rang. She indicated to her husband that she was going to step out to take the call. He gave her a good-natured wave and sunk back into his pillows.

"Mrs. Durham? Susan?" The voice on the other end was hesitant, but strong and deep. And familiar.

"This is RJ Peace," he continued. Susan placed a hand on heart and looked around for a chair to sit in.

"Yes, RJ," she said. Her calm tone was exactly the opposite of what she was feeling.

"Susan, I've been giving this thing a lot of thought," RJ said. "I've talked it over a lot with my wife, and my sister, too, and we feel it's the right thing to do."

"Yes?" Susan felt light-headed. She chewed on a nail.

"I've decided to be tested," RJ said slowly. "If it turns out that I'm a match, I will donate the bone marrow your husband needs."

"Thank God," Susan murmured. "Thank God."

She realized she was only half listening as RJ Peace discussed details and conditions. Susan forced down her elation so that she could concentrate. RJ wanted the process to be as anonymous as possible. He did not want his mother to know anything.

"She's still grieving my father," RJ said. "Learning about Jerome right now would be too upsetting for her."

Susan agreed. Contrary to what Lewis, Jr., thought about her, telling RJ and Albertina about Jerome had not been easy. Their recently departed father had still been a hero in their eyes until the Durhams had come along to shatter that myth. In her mind's eye, Susan saw Hattie's picture in its frame on the mantelpiece. "Damn you, Mother Durham," Susan thought to herself.

She shook it off and continued to hear RJ out. He didn't want to meet Jerome until and unless the match was absolutely proven. Later, he would consider a meeting, but, right now, he thought it might be a bit much for both of them. Susan agreed to that condition as well. Given the havoc that Hattie Durham had created in the family with her secrets, Susan could certainly understand why RJ would not be eager to open up a painful, hidden chapter from his father's past.

RJ told her he already had an appointment with his own doctor and that they would inform Jerome's medical team to determine the compatibility between the vital cells of the two men. A further matching meant RJ Peace could ultimately save Jerome's life.

"You don't know what this means to me, Mr. Peace," Susan said. "What it means to our whole family. Thank you so much." Silent tears ran down her face, tracking her makeup.

"Don't thank me yet," RJ said. "Wait until we get the test results." Susan was struck by the fact that even his voice sounded like Jerome's. There could be no doubt that the two men were brothers.

"**A**ll right, Susan. This all isn't just a coincidence. Tell me about this man. How did you find him?"

"Jerome, calm down, please, and I'll tell you more. You have got to reserve your strength." Susan pushed her husband gently back against his pillows and sat down next to him.

"When we found out that Lewis and Carl weren't compatible donors, I knew we had to find someone who was. Remember Lisa from the hospital? Believe it or not, she was a big help. She came when she heard about your situation. It turns out Mother Durham told her some things," Susan lowered her voice.

"What kind of things?" Jerome asked.

"About your real father. We confirmed it with Aunt Doe and then went looking for a man called Raymond Peace."

"Raymond Peace." Jerome repeated the name and frowned briefly. "Raymond. Ma'Dear was always calling me that. I guess now I know why."

"Yes, well, we found him. Sort of. He was your father," Susan paused. "I'm sorry to tell you this, but he passed away recently, honey," Susan said tenderly. "I'm sorry, Jerome. But it turns out he had children, two of them. We spoke to his son and told him about you. And now it sounds like he wants to try and help you."

"I have another brother, wow," Jerome said. "And he would do this for me? I want to meet him. This is unbelievable."

"His name is RJ, and I think he wants to meet you too, someday," Susan said. "But he wants to keep this low profile. His mother doesn't know about this, and he doesn't want her to find out."

"Oh." Jerome paused. He chided himself for being so selfish that he had not thought about what the Peace family might be going though.

"The situation is sensitive for them, the same way it has been for this family," Susan reassured him. "You'll have a lifetime to get to know your new brother, so, for now, we'll just accept his gift and get you better."

CHAPTER 18

The results turned out to be positive and conclusive: RJ Peace was declared to be a likely compatible match for Councilman Jerome Durham. Arrangements were made for RJ Peace to give his donation and recover at his local hospital, and the cells were transported a few cities over to Sharon Hill, where Jerome received his treatments. Susan had to scramble to keep the news out of the papers.

The Durhams rejoiced as Jerome's body readily accepted the genetic material of the brother he had never known.

Susan sent flowers and cards to the Peace residence, being carefully discreet in what was said on the cards. In addition to the bright table arrangement she had sent for the house, she also sent a delicate bedside arrangement for Lullah Peace. The flowers caught Lullah's eye the minute her daughter brought it into her room. The sympathies that had come in after Raymond's death had slowed down considerably.

Albertina told her mother they were from a well wisher and surprised the Durhams with a long, cordial letter. Susan surprised herself even more by taking up an ongoing correspondence with Albertina, who was clearly both intelligent and lonely. She was proud to know she was sister to one of the most prominent black men in the state, and she enjoyed reading details about his exciting campaign.

Albertina Peace had long been fascinated with the cultural history of the state and had collected clippings about Jerome Durham's political career long before she'd known he was his brother. Now, she followed every bit of available news about Jerome and Susan, and her letters were full of admiration and encouragement. Susan basked in the praise, since, nowadays, she was mainly the one who got photographed and interviewed by reporters.

One day, she came home from an informal debate, literally shaking with her triumph. She had reduced his opponent, Ted Lawson, to shreds.

He had come after her from the beginning, taking low shots at Jerome for being too weak to show up and allowing his wife to take the heat for him. Susan refused to lower herself to his level and surprised him by meeting each point he made with statistics and facts that turned the arguments in favor of the Durham candidacy. Her final rebuttal contained a statement that she was especially proud of, as it summed up what her husband's campaign while subtly criticizing Lawson.

"Jerome Durham's proposals include plans for revitalizing the neglected neighborhoods in this city in a way that will raise the value of the city to everyone. He's not just a small-detail man but a big picture visionary. Every one of his ideas incorporates ways to make our little town into a vital, more important part of our great state."

The audience had burst into surprised, enthusiastic applause for her as she exited the stage.

Jerome was going to be so proud of her. She couldn't wait to get home to see him. Victories like this really got her motor running. But when she called his phone, she got his voicemail, and, when she got home, she was surprised to find Jerome already in bed, asleep. Susan closed her eyes, squeezing back tears of disappointment.

She had really wanted to celebrate this evening in her husband's arms. It was still early, and she was still so keyed up she didn't know what to do with herself. She poured herself a drink and sat down slowly on the couch. After a few sips, Susan sat straight up and reached for purse. Her fingers trembled as she fished out the business card Craig Lancet had given her.

She looked at it for a few minutes and then downed her drink, relying on the liquor to give her the courage she needed to take the next step. Now that she had decided what to do, there was no turning back. She dialed the number. He picked up on the first ring.

"Yes, hello. Is this Craig Lancet?"

"Yes?"

"It's Susan Durham. I hope I did not catch you at a bad time."

"Yes, Mrs. Durham?" he said. His voice seemed filled with genuine pleasure. "I thought it was you. I would recognize that charming voice of yours anywhere."

Susan wasn't sure what she thought of that. She usually worked hard to disguise her accent, though she was aware traces of it could sneak back at times, especially when she was nervous, which she certainly was now after brazenly dialing Craig Lancet's phone in search of god only knew what.

"Please, call me Susan. I thought we discussed that," she laughed, attempting to cover her nerves.

"Yes, we did. Susan it is, then." Craig's chuckle helped her feel more at ease. "Mrs. Durham" sounded old, and that was the last thing she wanted to be reminded of as she struck up a flirtation with a man twenty years her junior. "What can I do for you, Susan?"

His voice sounded like honey as he emphasized her name. Susan could imagine how Craig looked standing there, with his pale blonde hair ruffled and maybe the collar of his shirt unbuttoned as he prepared to turn in for the night. She sucked in her breath at the thought.

"You said I should call if there was ever anything I thought you could do for me," she began. She could picture him raising his eyebrows at the unexpected request. He would have the phone in one hand and a drink in the other. She wondered how those hands would feel around her waist.

Craig Lancet's eyebrows had indeed shot up, with a sense of smug satisfaction that would have greatly offended Susan had she been aware of it. He had hoped she would call eventually; in fact, he had been sure that she would. He just hadn't expected it to be so soon.

The question now was whether Susan Durham would come right out and ask for what she wanted or if she would tiptoe around the issue. Women usually wanted it to seem like they were being seduced, rather than the ones who did the seducing. The fact was, it really was the other way around. Susan knew exactly what she was doing, with her honey-sweet Louisiana drawl and cool grey gaze. She was still an attractive woman, and it wasn't hard to imagine the beauty that must have carried her through her youth.

"I did say that," he said. "You're going to have to help me, though, because I can't imagine what that 'something' might be." Craig chuckled again. Whatever she needed him to do, he was up for it.

"Welllll," Susan said slowly. The liquor made her bold, but it had also had a calming effect on her. Now that she had settled down, she was shocked by what she was doing. But it was too late to turn back now. Susan realized she needed to think things through before going through with her plan. It was just a little hasty. It was just a little too soon. But there was no doubt in her mind there would be more nights like this. More nights to spend alone after carrying Jerome's weight for him, only to come home to find him dead asleep and snoring. More nights filled with compliments from strangers about how beautiful she was, only to have her efforts go unnoticed by a husband who was too weak to care.

That was it. She hated to even think the word, but she could no longer deny the truth: It wasn't his fault, but Jerome's strength and vitality, everything she loved most about him, was gone. Jerome Durham had become weak.

"Susan, are you still there?"

"Yes, I am, Craig. I'm still here. And it's too late tonight, and I must admit I'm exhausted, but I was wondering ... I wonder if I can see you again. Maybe this weekend?"

The following night, at Jerome's request, they had Reverend Solomon and his wife, Kelly, over for dinner. The couple had only been married for just over a year. Jerome had grown up and gone to school with them both. Susan enjoyed being the perfect hostess who could control the small talk over dinner. Jerome had indicated he needed some time to talk with Rodney Solomon alone, and Susan was uncomfortable being left alone with Kelly Solomon, so she invited the in-laws over for dessert. Carl and Junior settled down in front of the TV, while Jerome and the reverend excused themselves for a moment and disappeared into the study.

Later, after everyone had left, Jerome sat Susan down.

"Baby, before I say what I have to say, I want you to know how much I appreciate everything that you've done for me these past few years. Without you, I wouldn't be anywhere close to where I've come," Jerome began.

Susan grew immediately suspicious. "Come on out with it, Jerome," she said. "What are you trying to say?"

"You know me so well, don't you?" Jerome shook his head. He drew in a deep breath and took her hands in his. "I've decided to pull out of the mayor's race. I'm suspending the campaign."

Susan stared at Jerome. She put her hands to her

temples and shook her head. "Tell me I'm not hearing this. You can't be serious." She smoothed her hair back with her fingers, stood up and began to pace.

Jerome was a little surprised at Susan's reaction. He knew she would be upset, but he told himself that once she got over her initial shock and took his health into consideration, she would see this was the only decision that made sense. In fact, Susan should have been the one to ask him to quit the race, knowing how debilitating his treatment regimen would be. But Jerome knew his wife wanted him to become mayor, for his reasons as well as her own. Susan's ambition was endless.

"After all we've done, Jerome? After all the hard work? We've got people at the office now, churning out phone calls and flyers, and you just want to quit?" She paced the small space in front of him with folded arms. "If it's because of your health ..."

"That is the main reason why, yes, Susan," Jerome said. His own tone was clipped now, as his anger with her began to grow. Did she have no mercy regarding his condition whatsoever?

"Believe me, I know how I must sound to you, Jerome. But you can't let this thing scare you. Not now." Susan tried for a more reasonable tone, though inside she was nearing hysteria. "The treatment is starting to take effect, Dr. Mathieson said so. We just have to give it time."

"The city doesn't have time to wait for me to get back to 100 percent, my love," Jerome said, trying to calm her down. "It's not fair to ask anyone to do that."

"But you've still got me. I can keep helping out like I've

been doing and I can take on more, too! I will continue to cover for you while you're recovering. Didn't Roosevelt's wife run for months without anyone knowing it while her husband was incapacitated from a stroke?" Susan continued frantically. Jerome laughed gently.

"I'll bet you could run the country, like clockwork," he said, wrapping his arms around her waist. "Besides, Susan, you know that's not me. I would never purposely deceive the people about something as serious as my health."

"Did Reverend Solomon talk you into this?" she said.

Susan knew some folks in that church were jealous of her and Jerome. After dinner, Trudy had admired the new tea service, and Kelly Solomon had made some comment or other about the "trappings of power" that Susan was not sure had not been directed at her. If the Right Reverend Rodney Solomon had been in Jerome's ear about stepping out of the race, his wife had probably put him up to it.

But Jerome shook his head. "It was my idea," he said. "I've been thinking about it for a long time. I just asked Rodney for his advice."

"And just what was his advice?" Susan leaned against her husband's shoulder. She still couldn't believe he planned to discontinue his run for office.

"Rodney advised me to listen to my heart on this. I've been thinking about it, and what I really feel is that I wouldn't be able to do a damn thing to address the problems in this city if I can't address the problems in my own family."

"I understand that, Jerome, but can't you work on

both of those things at once?" Susan still held out the hope of talking him out of his plan.

Jerome kissed his wife's hands and clasped them to his heart. He fixed his golden gaze on her eyes, forcing her to look at him.

"Not if my health is a factor too, Susan," he said. "When I was a younger man, I might have had the energy to take all of this on at once. But we're all getting up there in years, and I'm recovering from an illness that might have killed me. I had to set my priorities, and my family and my health beat out the mayoral race this time."

Susan turned away so that Jerome would not see her expression.

"It is really hard for me to even say this, but Ma'Dear tore this family apart with the things she did," he said. "It doesn't even matter that I never knew Raymond Peace, any more than either of them did. We used to be like the three musketeers, and, now, Carl doesn't even want to say that I'm his brother anymore." Jerome was worked up to the point where there were tears in his eyes. "And I know Junior still thinks you had something to do with Ma'Dear dying, and that gives them even more reason to be mad with me. We've all been hurt by this thing, and I'm tired of it."

"So you're just going to give up everything because of it?" said Susan, slowly pulling away from him.

"If I'm not running for mayor, that will take my official position out of the equation. Nobody will be able to say I think I'm better than them because I hold office. You now that's been one of Carl's problems with me. And I'll have time to put into something we can do as a family.

Something we're all invested in. I know my brothers. If we're in business together, we'll be able to spend time together, and, eventually, we will talk things through," Jerome said.

"I don't know, Jerome. You know money and family don't always mix, and it's especially not going to work if one of your proposed business partners is already mad at you," Susan said. Right now Jerome's decisions were being driven by emotion, and she had to get him to listen to reason. He frowned and shook his head.

"Maybe you're right about that, but I still think this is what I want to do. Just can't rush into it," he said, more to himself than to her. "But I can still build towards it."

Susan realized that her husband had made up his mind and that fighting it now wouldn't do her any good. The thing to do now was to quiet him down and get him to put off making an announcement. Maybe a little time would bring the man to his senses.

"You know I'll support you in whatever you want to do, honey," she said sweetly. "But you don't have to announce anything just this minute. Sleep on it a day or two, and get your thoughts together so that we can do things right."

Jerome's smile of relief was like the sunshine. Knowing that Susan wasn't going to fight him on this thing made it so much easier. She went up on tiptoe, kissed him on the cheek, and left the room. Jerome went over to the mirror and straightened his collar. It was going to be a beautiful day.

CHAPTER 20

J erome's announcement had left Susan dumbstruck, but it had immediately sparked an idea so outrageous she thought it just might work. He dropped his bombshell on the stunned staff at HQ, but she gave them no time to react.

"Listen up, everybody," she said, clapping her hands to get their attention. "Jerome may have decided to drop his bid for mayor, but I have no intention of wasting all of the hard work that's been done by the Durham for Mayor campaign staff," she said. "I have decided to pick up where my husband is leaving off and declare my candidacy for mayor."

Susan looked around, enjoying the surprised expressions on everyone's faces.

"I don't know if I'm the only one, but I don't think that's such a good idea," Donetta said.

"We haven't done any exploratory research," someone else murmured. Susan scowled. The office had started to buzz. Jerome raised his hand to silence everyone.

"Susan," he intervened gently. "There's no doubt in my mind that you would make a terrific mayor, but I think Donetta's right. The timing is not great. This is one case where your inexperience would work against you. Believe me, Ted Lawson and his supporters would jump all over that."

"We didn't get the chance to find out if this city is ready for a black candidate, much less one who's female and black," Donetta said.

"It would be an uphill battle," Jerome agreed.

"We don't have time for exploratory research," the nervous intern repeated.

Susan didn't have a response to their perfectly logical objections. But she wasn't going to concede that easily. Before she had a chance to say anything, Donetta spoke up again.

"What about city council? There's no reason why you shouldn't run for the seat Jerome is vacating," she said. Everyone was silent for a moment. Jerome beamed.

"Donetta, that's a brilliant idea," he said. He leaned over and kissed his sister-in-law on the cheek. "That just might work."

"I think you'd stand a better chance," Donetta said, emboldened by Jerome's support. "Jerome's key constituents already know who you are."

"As the wife of the elected official who currently holds the seat, you are intimately familiar with the issues I've been working on," Jerome said. "You could run on a platform of continuation."

"I'll bet you would get automatic support from the black churches and several neighborhood groups who voted for Uncle Jerome and love him, just like we do," said one of the staff.

"I don't know," Susan said. "I'll have to think about it."

"Don't think too long," Donetta warned. "I'm sure the deadline for filing your intention is close."

"We'll get back to you soon, Donetta," Susan said

dismissively. "Jerome and I have got to talk about this more in private."

Secretly, Susan loved the idea, but she was unwilling to give her sister-in-law credit for coming up with it. She took Jerome's arm and started to lead him toward the inner office.

"It's never too soon to start drafting an announcement speech for Mrs. Durham and an endorsement speech for me," Jerome called back over his shoulder.

The take-charge tone in his voice made Susan ache for a moment. He would have made such an excellent mayor. But that pang of regret could not dampen her own growing excitement.

CHAPTER 21

The doctors had explained that Jerome's ongoing treatment would negatively affect his energy levels and consequently, his sex drive. Susan understood. But understanding a thing and experiencing it are two different things.

Like so many other nights, Susan had come home excited after a day of hearing people say how poised and capable she was. She expected Jerome to agree with their compliments, smother her with kisses, and lead her up the stairs or maybe take her right there on the living room couch. Instead, Jerome would smile and listen politely as she recounted the day's events, but soon he would beg off, and she would find him later, napping, poring over his business plans, or talking on the phone with Junior or Rodney Solomon.

Susan had had it. Tonight was one too many nights of having Jerome discourage her advances. She told him she had forgotten something at the office and that she would probably stay and work for a few hours in order to make up for the lost time. She nearly panicked when he offered to go with her but managed to maintain her cool.

"I won't hear of it, honey," she told her husband firmly. "Your immune system is already compromised enough as it is without you going out in this chilly night air." She assured him that the security guards would walk her to and from her car at the office and that she would call when she was on her way home.

Jerome raised his eyebrows slightly. Susan had showered and changed into fresh clothes. She put on perfume and combed her hair as carefully as if it were morning and she was just going into the office for the first time. But Susan was always meticulous and often showered several times a day, joking that soap and water freshened one's mind as much as it did one's body. He held her coat for her and walked her to her car, kissing her on the cheek before closing the door of her sedan.

Susan waved goodbye to her husband and watched him grow smaller in her rearview mirror as she drove away. Once she'd turned the corner and gotten out of sight, she pulled over to the curb and pulled out her phone. She redialed a number and waited with growing anticipation as the phone rang.

"Hello, Craig?"

Half an hour later, the two were alone in a hotel room. Susan had tied a scarf over her hair and wore dark glasses, hoping to disguise her appearance should anyone see them. But things were quiet at that hour and she managed to go unnoticed. She trembled with anticipation as Craig helped her remove her jacket. He kissed her gently as he helped her unbutton the ivory silk blouse that closely matched her skin. Susan turned around modestly to step out of her skirt, hanging it on the back of her chair. When she turned back to face Craig, he stood there with his shirt unbuttoned, watching her undress. She looked beautiful standing there in her beige slip and heels. Her gingerbread-dark hair was tinted with gold highlights from the sun that obscured the gray she'd accumulated.

But when Craig stepped to her, she pulled away.

"Could I have some more wine?" she asked.

Craig smiled. "Of course."

She picked up the plastic champagne glass and held it up, laughing nervously as he poured a glass for her and a glass for himself. He sat down on the bed and patted the spot next to him. She joined him, taking a long sip of wine before pausing to remove her shoes.

"Thank you, Craig," she said. "I guess I'm a little nervous."

"Of course you are," he said smoothly. "A true lady would be before an intimate moment, I would think."

"You know, you're nothing like your Uncle Chancelly was," Susan mused. "Other than looking almost exactly like him, which you do."

"How do you mean?"

"Chance was much more brash and insistent," she said. "I suppose that was because he was so young. You've had time to grow into your confidence and all your wealth and your class. Time to become a gentleman."

Susan took another sip of wine, then put the glass down as a chill ran through her. Describing the difference between uncle and nephew had brought her to a sudden realization. Craig saw her shiver and put his hands on her shoulders.

"You're cold," he said. He stood up and folder the covers down. "Here, why don't we slip into bed and warm each other up."

Craig started to remove his shirt and Susan stepped

forward to place a hand on his chest, with a slight pressure that was not inviting, halting him.

"What?" Craig was confused.

"I just realized I can't do this," Susan said. She stepped away and began gathering her clothes.

"What happened? I thought we wanted each other," Craig said.

"I thought it was what I wanted, but now I realize it's just a bad idea, Craig. Forgive me."

Clutching her clothes to her chest, she rushed past him into the bathroom and closed and locked the door. Her thoughts raced furiously as she hurried into her suit. What the hell was I thinking? *You can't get back the past,* Susan scolded herself. *Craig Lancet may look like his uncle, but he's not. And being with Craig wouldn't make me the innocent girl I was before I met Chance. It wouldn't make me anything but the cheap whore Eleanor Foster thinks I am anyway. The last think I want to do is prove that old bitch right.*

Susan snapped her leather gloves on with determination. She looked at herself in the mirror and set her chin, determined to walk out of the situation with dignity.

Craig stood up from the chair as she came out of the bathroom. She saw he had buttoned up his shirt, and left his tie hanging over his shoulders.

"I'll walk you to your car," he said.

"No, thank you," Susan responded politely. "I don't want to chance anyone seeing us together." She checked herself in the full length mirror on the back of the door. Everything was in place.

"You really are a charming man, Craig Lancet. I wish you the best, and I do want to thank you for everything. You made me feel like a teenager again," she said. "But now I've come back to my senses again. I have to get home to my husband." She leaned forward and gave him a quick kiss on the cheek before rushing from the room.

Out in the hallway, Susan quickly slid on a pair of dark sunglasses. She hustled to straighten her clothes as she waited for an elevator, eyes darting from side to side to make sure no one saw her. She waited impatiently as the car slowly made its way down to the lobby. Susan was relieved that no one had joined her for the ride. Her heart was beating fast and loud. She needed the moment alone to compose herself.

When she stepped off of the elevator, she looked around for the quickest way out without going through the library. There were side entrances on either side of the hall, so she headed for the one nearest the parking lot. She stepped out of the door and stopped short.

A few spaces down a tall, lean man had just gotten out of his car and was opening the passenger door for his companion, an almost equally tall, impossibly long-legged woman. He grinned, whispered something to her, and took her by the arm to lead her into the hotel. Lewis! Susan's eyes widened in recognition.

What's he doing here? And who was that woman? Susan stifled her gasp of shock and ducked her head so that they wouldn't see her. This was a mystery she couldn't solve at the moment, as she surely had her own problems to deal with. She waited as they headed for the entrance, then hurriedly ran for her car.

Several floors up, alone in the room Susan had exited quickly, Craig Lancet stood at the window buttoning his cuffs. He saw her get in her car and drive away like a bat out of hell.

"So long, Susan," he said. His smile turned cruel as he finished dressing before the mirror. "For now."

CHAPTER 22

The smell of Trudy Durham's chicken dumpling stew filled the kitchen. Trudy stood before the stove stirring the pot. She heard the sound of her husband, Carl, stumbling down the stairs. He had already started drinking. She hoped she could convince him to stay in and stay out of trouble. Soon, he made his way into the kitchen.

"That smells good," Carl grunted as he fell into a chair.

"Mmm-hmm," said Trudy, glancing over her shoulder at him. "It's Baby Brother's favorite. I thought I'd take some over to him and Susan. Lord knows that girl must be so tired." Trudy moved back and forth carrying out little kitchen tasks. She did not see the thunderous shadow creep into Carl's expression at the mention of Jerome.

"The man has bone cancer, not a cold," said Carl, folding his arms in mockery of her. Alerted by his tone, Trudy glanced at Carl again cautiously. She tried to determine whether it was better to ignore his comment.

"Well, anyway, it's his favorite, so I thought I'd take them some, but, of course, it's one of your favorites, too, sugar," she said. "Why don't I fix you a bowl? I've got some hot cornbread here, coming fresh out of the oven."

Trudy turned away and busied herself with preparing a plate for her husband. Carl's eyes narrowed, growing smaller and meaner as she sat his food in front of him and then turned back to the stove, where she poured most of the stew into a Tupperware container and wrapped up half of the cornbread. Carrying his bowl, Carl followed her out of the house. "I'm just going to drop this off. I won't be long," Trudy said.

"Stay as long as you like," Carl muttered. "In fact, you can stay over there forever, for all I care."

He caught Trudy completely off guard by first hurling his bowl into the yard, then stalking back into the house and slamming the door.

"Carl!"

Trudy ran back up the steps in time to hear him sliding the bolt on the door. He had locked her out.

"Carl Benton Durham, I don't know what you think you're doing." Trudy banged on the door. She could see him through the window, laughing at her while he drank from a half-full bottle of whisky. She watched him as he walked into the living room and looked at the pictures arranged on the mantel. He picked up his mother's photograph and looked at it for a moment. Then he walked over to the china cabinet. When Hattie died, Trudy and Carl had inherited the beautiful old antique and the collection of delicate, expensive china and bric-a-brac that she had kept in it. An old pistol that had belonged to her was locked in the bottom drawer.

"Carl, what are you doing?"

Carl had taken his keys out of his pocket and was examining the keys, one by one. He was trying to find the key to the drawer. Panicking now, Trudy banged on the door some more. Her efforts were in vain. Her husband was ignoring her. Holding Hattie's picture tightly to his chest, Carl leaned over to unlock the drawer.

"Oh, my God." Trudy ran back to the car, where she had placed her purse along with the food for Jerome. She scrambled in her bag for her cell phone. Tears blurred her sight as she scrolled in search of a number that she finally dialed by memory.

"Hello? This is Trudy Durham. Can you come over here now, please, and quick? It's Carl. It's Carl," she repeated breathlessly, running back up the steps. She could no longer see Carl in the living room, but she could hear him moving around in there, singing some drunken song. "He's gone completely out of control. I'm not sure what set him off, but he locked me out of the house, and I'm afraid he's going to hurt himself if somebody doesn't stop him. Come quick. Please!"

The scene at Carl and Trudy Durham's house was pure chaos as Reverend Rodney Solomon drove up. Trudy was outside, crying. Reverend Solomon could see Carl pacing back and forth in the master bedroom upstairs. The window was open.

Carl paused and threw something out. Glass shattered on the sidewalk belong, joining a growing pile of broken bric-a-brac.

"It's Mother Durham's fine china," Trudy sobbed. "Carl doesn't want it in the house anymore. He says he doesn't want anything that belonged to her anymore."

Something else came spinning out the window into the air, nearly hitting the reverend before crash landing on the ground at his feet. It was Hattie Durham's portrait, now distorted through the broken glass.

"Carl, stop it!" Trudy wailed. Neighbors had started to gather and stare at the spectacle. Carl threw more china.

"Carl, it's Rodney," Reverend Solomon called up to him. "I want to talk to you."

"Pastor Solomon, you knew my mother, Hattie," Carl hollered down. "I bet you didn't know she was a liar or a cheater or a killer." The neighbors gasped. Trudy wailed her embarrassment.

"Now, Carl Durham, you know that wasn't called for,"

Reverend Solomon called sternly. "I want to come up and talk to you. Now, will you let me in?"

After a moment, Carl disappeared from the window, presumably to go downstairs and open the door. Rodney quickly called his wife, and asked her to locate Donetta and bring her over to Carl and Trudy's. "You can probably get her at the campaign office," he said, heading briskly up the walk. He stopped only to pat Trudy encouragingly on the back. A neighbor placed her hands around Trudy's shoulders and led her further away.

When Carl answered the door, Reverend Solomon noted his condition. He had never seen the man looking so bad. He was unshaven and smelled drunk. He saw how Rodney was looking at him and looked down in embarrassment.

"Come in, Reverend," he said, with a shaky welcoming gesture. Rodney Solomon could not help shaking his head as he entered the home, and Carl quickly closed and bolted the door behind him.

"Carl, what kind of a man locks his wife out of her own house?" he said. "You need to let Sister Trudy come in."

"Not until I talk to you first," said Carl, speaking slowly and carefully. He was ashamed at being drunk in front of this family friend.

"All right. Let's sit down and talk. Show me into the kitchen, and I'll make us some coffee," Reverend Solomon said.

"All right, Rev," Carl grinned agreeably. Rodney clapped the man on the back and walked him into the kitchen.

"Now, to answer your question back there, yes, I remember Mother Durham well," Reverend Solomon said as he sat down with his coffee. "Man, she was always fussing over your little brother, wasn't she?" Carl grimaced, not needing at that moment to be reminded of the way Hattie had favored Jerome. But the reverend was on a roll.

"You would think she would have been good at snipping apron strings once Rome came along, seeing as how she had you and Lewis, Jr., to practice on," the reverend said. "But I can remember times we had to beg her to let the boy even come out on the porch to shoot marbles."

"Yeah, well, he got bad sick that one time, and I guess once was enough," said Carl, thinking that Hattie had been that way over Jerome since the day he was born, not just since he had gotten sick. Overprotective. If anything, Jerome's boyhood illness had made Hattie's protectiveness even worse.

"She loved all of y'all, though," the reverend said agreeably. "Come to think of it, she loved all children, didn't she? What was that she used to say all the time? 'Every child deserves to be loved.' Something like that."

"Yes. Do you think she really believed that?" Carl asked. Reverend Solomon looked at him.

"Yes, Carl, I do think your mother believed that every child deserved to be loved," he said. "But I don't think she just meant that literally. That is to say, she wasn't just referring to the very young."

"I think when she said 'child' your mama meant 'child of God,' like she was saying that everybody deserved to be love. Not just certain folks. Not just perfect folks," Reverend Solomon nodded. "In a lot of ways, I think she was really talking about herself."

"What do you mean?"

"Carl Durham, your mother was a very deep woman. She didn't say a whole lot, but she struck me as a person who had a whole lot going on, you know? Seemed to me she was trying to work things out between God and herself, and she was trying to remind herself that she had a place in His divine plan just like everybody else."

"You picked all that up from my ma?" Carl was astonished. Rodney Solomon had been observant, and even wiser and more mature as a little boy than Carl had thought.

Carl remembered Hattie had often refused to let Jerome hang out with other kids for fear something might happen to him. But if Rodney Solomon was there, she didn't hesitate. Carl knew Ma'Dear thought young Rodney had a special calling, and that, if he was there, then Jerome was safe.

"Your mama had a strong way of loving about her that you could feel," Reverend Solomon said. "There was a sense of purpose in that woman. I always got the feeling she was searching for something."

"Yeah, well we found out she was searching for something all right," Carl said. "Or someone. Someone other than my father." He folded his arms.

"Carl, is that what this is about? Your mother having another man's baby?"

"She killed him."

"What?"

"I said she killed him. She told me herself. And now I

know she did it so that she could have her baby from this man, Raymond Peace." Carl buried his face in his hands.

"My mother was not the sweet, innocent little old lady that you think you remember so well," he said bitterly. Reverend Solomon took a deep breath.

"Who among us is perfect?" the reverend intoned. "Who among us can cast the first stone? Carl, man, how can I assure you, you don't have to feel responsible for anything your mother did – but neither does your brother, Jerome. Those were her sins and her choices," Rodney said. "It's not up to us to judge her. And in her life didn't she do some good things too? Make some good choices? Look at you and your brothers."

The reverend held Carl's gaze. "You are good men, all of you. Good people. She tried to teach you to make good choices. And didn't she try to teach you all to stick together, no matter what?"

"Maybe she was trying to prepare you all for this very thing, this very day when you would need to make some hard choices," Reverend Solomon said. He patted Carl's back. "Listen, brother, maybe we can't know your mother's reasons for doing things we don't understand or agree with, but I'll tell you what you can do: You can hold on to the good things she left you with – and that's your brothers. Both of them."

Carl remained silent, thinking about everything Reverend Solomon had just said.

"Reverend, I'm glad you here. It's overdue, but I always did mean to thank you and the others for what you did for Jerome," Carl said. "It meant a lot to him to have you all come see him and pray for him like you did."

"Jerome's a brother to us all, and, of course, we wanted to show our support," Reverend Solomon said. "It was our honor."

"Well, seeing as how we got such good news right after that, I'd say it worked," Carl grinned. He felt like a weight had been lifted from his shoulders. He was surprised to realize how relieved he really was that his younger brother was getting better. It wasn't Jerome's fault that Hattie had favored him. What she had done to Carl's and Junior's father wasn't Jerome's fault either. Nothing Hattie had done was Jerome's fault, and her feelings for the favorite didn't mean she loved his brothers any less. Nor did it mean that they couldn't go on supporting one another; they needed to do that now more than ever.

Carl shook the reverend's hand. "So, thank you again."

Reverend Solomon grinned back. "The prayers don't stop here. Your whole family continues to be in our thoughts. Now, let's get back out there, and let Trudy in. That woman has been worried sick about you – and I suspect she's got some cleaning up for you to do."

CHAPTER 24

Donetta was in her kitchen when she heard someone pounding on the front screen door. She walked through the house and saw Gloria Ricks standing there.

"Donetta, girl, come out here, and look at this bag I just bought!" Gloria squealed. Donetta stepped out of the screen door.

"Look at this!" Gloria proudly displayed a tan leather swing bag with adorned with a leather and brass buckle shaped like a flower.

"That is cute," Donetta said.

"Girl, they are selling these knockoffs on a corner up there by Merrington and Vine. Do you want to go up there now, and see what they have left before they sell out?" Gloria was ready to race out of there.

"No, I don't think so," Donetta said. She loved shopping, and she was a sucker for a good deal.

"Well, I'll tell you what, girl," Gloria said. "I don't think you want to miss this because not only did that vendor have great bags this morning, it also had a great view of a certain tall, dark, and chocolate man when I was there." She looked at Donetta meaningfully, as if talking that way about the woman's husband to her face was an everyday thing.

Donetta didn't feel like playing Gloria's games.

"You trying to tell me you saw Junior in town? So what, the man has places to go and people to see."

"It ain't no thing, girl," Gloria said. "I just thought Lewis went for shorter women with a little more meat on their bones." She looked Donetta up and down, then looked down at her own curvaceous body.

"This chick he was with was the long and skinny type. He must have felt like being the one to climb the ladder for a change." She waited for Donetta to pick up on her provocative words, but, so far, Donetta was refusing the bait.

"Gloria," Donetta said, "that man ain't got no particular type, ok? As long as it's a woman, it's his type. But I'm his wife, and I know him. His bark is worse than his bite, and, at the end of the day, he always comes home to me." She held up her chin. It was time to let Gloria know just who was the queen bee. "Anyway, the man is a commercial real estate broker. That means he has to meet with all kinds of people to do business. All shapes and sizes."

"Well, this one definitely had a shape ... and a size to her, too." Gloria outlined the shape of an hourglass with her hands, stretched an arm upwards to indicate Bev Epperson's extreme height, then burst into laughter. "Come on, Donetta, girl. I'm just trying to lighten things up, not trying to make trouble between you and your man."

"No trouble," Donetta replied. Her voice was cool, though her heart was pounding. She wasn't about to let on to Gloria how worried she really was. Gloria looked skeptical. Her pride was hurt because of her failure to pull Lewis Durham away from his wife.

"Well, if you're sure you don't want to go," she said. "These bags are so cute, I just might pick me up another one." She scooted back towards her car, swinging her bag.

After Gloria drove off, Donetta thought for a minute, weighing her options. Then, she hopped into her own car. She had some serious recon of her own to do.

Meanwhile, Susan was at home, bent over her desk, sorting through a pile of letters. She was separating them into two piles: one for general comments that did not necessarily require action, and one for more specific comments that called for something to be done. It never failed to surprise her how much hate mail they actually got. People could be very passionate about political races. Rather than respond directly to any of it, Susan tried to make sure that the campaign's actions addressed legitimate concerns in some way. She hoped that people would see something positive in their efforts. She was so consumed in the work that the phone startled her when it rang. She nearly jumped out of her seat. She was even more shocked when she found out who it was.

"Craig," she said uncertainly. "I didn't expect to hear from you ... so soon."

"Oh, Susan," he responded. "Are you talking about that awkwardness between us the other night? I hope that we can put it behind us. But I'm calling because I need to see you right away."

"Right now?" she said doubtfully.

"Let's say in an hour or so. That will give us time enough to meet at some suitable halfway point, won't it?"

Susan hesitated. It was broad daylight. She couldn't imagine what could be so urgent or where they could go where they wouldn't be seen. She told herself she was being silly. Of course, their behavior would be appropriate. Anyone who saw them would just assume she was meeting with a constituent or something.

"I'm kind of busy right now," she said. "Can't we make a date for later in the week?"

"This won't wait," Craig said. There was something in his tone that Susan didn't like, but she couldn't put her finger on it.

"All right," she said. She reluctantly put her things away and dressed quickly, but carefully, for the meeting. She wanted to appear as calm, professional, and chaste as possible. She checked her makeup in the mirror and realized for the first time how prominent the lines in her skin were becoming. She smoothed her fingers over her complexion and tried to compose her features before getting into her car.

Craig had suggested a small café for their meeting. Not many people were there, and Susan easily got a table. She ordered coffee and a small salad, and sat there waiting. She was far too nervous to eat.

Craig and his mother, Eleanor, came up behind her, so that she did not see them approach. As he led his mother around and she saw Susan's face, she started to walk away. His grip was firm as he practically wrestled her down into the chair by her arm.

"Hello, Susan," Craig said. His voice was as chilly as his smile was warm. "I believe you two know each other."

"Yes. Eleanor, it's certainly a surprise to see you again

so soon," Susan forced politeness into her tone. She glanced at Craig with irritation. He hadn't mentioned bringing his mother.

"Son, what is the meaning of this?" Eleanor pointedly ignored Susan. "I will not sit down at a table with this woman."

"Mother, sit," Craig said out of the side of his mouth; his polite smile barely moved.

"Have some coffee," said Susan, gesturing at the pot on the table. Some paper cups were stacked beside it.

"I believe I will," Craig said. "Mother?"

Eleanor shook her head emphatically. She continued to glare at Susan.

"No, thank you, son. I really don't believe I could stomach any refreshment right now," she said. "The sooner you state your business, the sooner we can leave this place." Eleanor's voice rose as she spat her words. People were looking at them.

"Mother, please, you're making a scene," Craig said.

"Your mother's right," Susan said. "Please just tell us why we're here before your mother passes out."

It was true, Eleanor Foster-Lancet appeared on the verge of hysteria. She clutched her purse and looked from side to side out of feverish eyes, panicked at the thought of being seen by someone they knew.

Craig smiled the lazy smile that had once made Susan's stomach flutter with desire. Now, it made her nauseous as she met his eyes and saw the coldness there.

"Well," he began. "I brought us all here together today in order to discuss a matter that is important to all of us. To you, Mrs. Durham, as the wife of a rising political star;

and to you, Mrs. Foster-Lancet, as the mother of the only living male heir to our family's fortune and great name."

Eleanor shook her head impatiently. "Son, what are you talking about? Please make your point." Craig continued to smile.

"Susan and I have become great friends, haven't we?" he said. "We've actually become quite close and cozy. One might even say intimate." Susan and Eleanor both gasped in horror.

"But then, suddenly, last week to my dismay," Craig continued, not giving them time for further reaction, "the councilman's lovely wife here decided that it was no longer in her best interest to maintain our friendship. She asked me to stop calling her and told me that she never wanted to see me again."

"Craig, this is outrageous," Susan whispered furiously. She met Eleanor's gaze and saw a gleam of malicious satisfaction there.

"It seems the woman came to her senses, Craig," said Eleanor, fussily arranging her gloves. "I certainly hope you came to yours, too, and agreed to end this nonsense."

"No, I haven't yet, but I'm hoping the two of you can help convince me," Craig said. He grinned. "After all, I do realize that it probably is in everyone's best interest that it come to an end between us, eh, Mrs. Durham?"

"What is it worth to you to protect your husband from a scandal like this? Can you imagine the headlines?" Craig turned to his mother. "And, Mother, can you?" She looked away, and he scoffed.

"I didn't think so," he said cruelly. He turned back to Susan. "So, you see, you're not alone in this after all,

Susan. I figure it's equally important to both of you that we end this thing and that we make sure nobody ever mentions it again. Nobody." He made a gesture with his fingers that Susan and Eleanor both understood; his silence was for sale.

"Craig, you're despicable," Susan hissed.

"Maybe so, but perhaps there is some redeeming quality in a man who wants to bring two enemies together. What better way to you two together than to have you share this burden? Each one of you is dependent on the other to make sure her family is protected." He looked between them both, smiling.

"Nothing happened between us. Besides, you can't prove anything." Susan tossed her head.

"I think I can provide enough details to make a nice satisfying story," Craig said. "How about a date, a time, and a place? Where did you tell your husband you were that night?" When Susan didn't respond, he leaned in even closer.

"How about I speak to a reporter about a certain piece of designer lingerie? Do you think your husband would recognize my description of that beautiful slip? And the way that heart-shaped mole on your lovely left shoulder shows through the lace?"

Eleanor looked away in distaste. Susan was speechless.

"Should I call for more coffee?" Craig said pleasantly. He did not wait for an answer, but signaled a waiter, who nodded and rushed off toward the kitchen.

"I'll leave you now to sort this out between yourselves," he said. "So, the two of you should talk. Try to come up with a figure that I'll like, and I'll consider the offer."

"Craig, you cannot be serious," Eleanor said. He ignored her.

"Let me help you get started with negotiations," he said. "Anything less than seven figures would be an insult, and you would be wasting your time even mentioning it to me."

The two women stared at him in disbelief. Craig smiled. "And don't take too long. Let's see, the end of the week should be plenty of time." He stood up and threw a few bills on the table for the coffee. "Susan, you can call me if you like, but I will certainly understand if you prefer to leave it up to my mother to make the transaction, given the circumstances. Mother, I'll see you later." He turned and left, whistling casually.

Susan and Eleanor stared at each other with undisguised hatred. Eleanor fussed with her gloves and stood up as if to leave just as the waiter returned with a fresh pot of coffee. Susan warmed her cup, then lifted the pot in a grim invitation to the white woman across the table from her. Eleanor hesitated, then shook her head. She sat back down.

S usan ran to her Benz and shut the door. She put her hands on the steering well and sat there, thinking frantically about what might be the cleanest, quickest way to get her hands on the cash she needed to pay off Craig Lancet. Was there any other way to deal with the situation? She wished she could kill the man with her bare hands, but that was just an impulsive thought, and she had to put her days of living by impulse behind her, for once and for all. Too many people in her past had become victims of her violent anger.

She had some money available due to the properties her father had left her, but not enough. At any rate, she was too cautious to make a bank transaction that would leave a paper trail. Even though her accounts were private, she didn't want any opportunity for questions to come up later about how such a large withdrawal vanished into thin air. Jerome might be distracted now, but there was always the possibility that he would notice later.

No, the money could not come out of the bank. There had to be another way. Susan tried to think from whom she could get the money from.

Over the years, she remained close to her sister Daisy, and they had stayed in touch, though infrequently. Daisy alone understood the need to keep their shared background a secret, as it was as important to her as it was to Susan, though not in the same way.

Any "darkness" in Daisy's genes had somehow been erased by her mother's blood and was virtually non-existent in the houseful of blonde, blue-eyed children she and her white husband produced.

Daisy was the only person from her past that Susan had notified about her marriage to Jerome. Of course, her loyal sister had been supportive.

"Susan Chalfont, you do not mean to tell me that after all of that courting by Chance Foster, you turned around and married a black man. Actually married one!" Daisy had giggled over a late night, long-distance phone call that would be paid for by her rich husband.

"Can you imagine my mother's face if she ever gets wind of this? But believe me, she won't be hearing it from me," Daisy continued. It had been her mother, Stella, who first suggested that Susan play up her European genes and blend in as a white girl. After all, her daughter had done so successfully. Stella told Susan to keep her hair light and advised her on what makeup to wear to enhance the paleness of her skin. She had thought she was doing the girl a favor.

The thought of how Stella would react to her daughter's half-sister marrying a black man was indeed a comical one. Susan giggled too.

"Even so, you got one of the good ones," Daisy went on. "I've seen your Jerome, on pictures and on TV, and he is ever so handsome and sincere," she gushed. "He's just the kind of man we need all politicians to be, black or white, even though they seldom are. You just be good to that man, Susan. And remember, he's lucky to have you, too."

Susan's eyes misted over as she thought about her sister. There was no doubt that Daisy would give her the money she needed, without hesitation or questions, and she could be counted on to be discreet. Yet, Susan's hand hesitated as she held her phone.

That was because, in her heart, she knew it would be wrong to bring Daisy into this. It would taint what was probably the only truly honest relationship that Susan had in her life, and it would take advantage of her sister's sweetness. Besides, her mistake in starting an affair with Craig was such a sordid topic, Susan couldn't imagine trying to explain it to her carefree, sunny sister. Susan turned away from the phone. She sat down, and raised a hand to her lips, ready to chew her nails. She realized there was only one thing to do.

CHAPTER 26

D onetta spotted Junior's car on the street outside of the café. She had driven past there several times the past week during the lunch hour, and, today, he was there, just as Gloria Ricks had said he would be. Donetta parked quickly and rushed into the café. As soon as she entered the place, she recognized her husband from the back. She would know Junior's lean, tall shape anywhere. He was in animated conversation with a thin, pretty, brown-skinned young woman in a suit. Her long legs were crossed at the knees, and she was riveted by whatever it was that Junior was saying. Moving quickly, Donetta approached before they realized it.

"Junior, who is this?"

Junior jumped to his feet.

"Donetta!" he said, clearly surprised.

"Mrs. Durham," Beverly said swiftly. Her smile was both pleasant and cautious as she extended her hand for Donetta to shake. "I'm Beverly Epperson. I'm pleased to meet you."

Junior stepped between them, putting a protective arm back towards Beverly and a shielding one toward Donetta. He was not about to let his wife cause a scene.

"Donetta, Beverly is my lawyer," he said. "She's helping me figure out how we can reopen Ma'Dear's case files." The look in his wife's eyes was a warning not to mess with her. Junior knew he had better nip the problem in the bud right now.

"Really?" Donetta said slowly. She narrowed her eyes skeptically, trying to discern whether he was lying. "I've been hearing about folks seeing you and some narrow-assed female all over town, Junior." She looked Beverly up and down. "This is her?"

Beverly Epperson was too professional to react to the insult. She picked up her briefcase and nodded to the couple.

"I'm going to leave and let you two talk," she said. "Mr. Durham, let me know if you want me to proceed." Beverly swiftly exited the restaurant, leaving the drama behind. As it unfolded, people at the surrounding tables pretended not to watch.

"Let's talk about this at home, Junior," Donetta said. She turned and walked out as well.

"Nothing's going on between me and Beverly Epperson but business," he called after her. Now, people around the restaurant looked up and stared openly, but Junior did not care. He really did love his wife, and he was not too proud to show it.

Donetta was already pulling out when he caught up to her in the parking lot. He waved her down, and she carefully slowed and pulled up next to him. He better be prepared to explain himself good, she thought. Junior leaned in the window.

"You sure you're all right to drive home, baby?" he asked.

"I'm cool," Donetta said, and she meant it. She wasn't

the kind of woman who flew out of control when she was upset. She wanted to believe Junior, but that lawyer chick was tall, pretty, and young. Definitely the type who could make another woman feel seriously insecure. Donetta found herself driving a little fast, as she was anxious to get home and settle the matter with her husband.

At the house, Junior pulled up to the curb and jumped out of the car, rushing into the house after Donetta. She had left the door open and stood in the living room with her arms folded.

"You believe me, don't you, Donetta?" he said. "Beverly Epperson is my lawyer, that's all."

"How come you never told me about her?" Donetta asked him. "I didn't even know you still wanted to go after Susan."

"I was going to tell you, Donetta," he said. Even he realized how lame that sounded. "When the time was right."

"It still seems like you were trying to keep me from finding out about that Epperson woman," Donetta said.

"I used to be that way, but, you've got to believe me, Donetta, I haven't been with any other woman in so long I can't even remember how long it's been," Junior said. He had to be careful with the way he said it, but his heart was sincere. "You changed my life, girl. I've been faithful to you."

"I don't know," Donetta hesitated.

"Please, just tell me what to do to prove myself to you, Donetta," Junior pleaded. His dark brown eyes begged. Donetta felt her heart melting, but she was determined to make her position clear to the man she loved.

"All right, then, Junior. You really want to prove you love me?" Donetta challenged. "You can drop this thing you got going against Susan," she said.

"What?" Junior was incredulous. "You cannot be serious."

"Yes, I am, Junior. Think about it. Prosecuting Susan won't bring your mother back, and it would kill your brother. He just survived a terrible illness, and you helped him fight for his life, just so you could destroy him by accusing his wife of murder. How does that sound?"

Donetta stopped and looked at Junior for a moment, trying to drive home her point. "You were willing enough to forgive Mother Durham when you learned what she did to your father. So, how is Susan any different?"

"Is it worth it to you to tear the woman your brother has loved all these years away from him now?" Donetta was drilling Junior with question after question. "And after how hard both you and Jerome have been fighting to get Carl to come back to the family, you plan to set off a bomb right in the middle of the family and tear us all apart by accusing Susan?"

"Dammit, Donetta," Junior moaned. He closed his eyes and clenched his fists. He didn't want to admit it, but the woman did make some kind of sense. *Dear Lord,* he thought, *I have to think about this.* "I don't see how doing this would prove I've been faithful to you. One has nothing to do with the other. I mean, I can get another lawyer if that's what this about."

"You telling me that you've been faithful is what proves it to me, Junior," Donetta said. "Your word has to be good enough for me since I really don't have anything else to go on. I have to trust you."

Donetta stood up on tiptoe and kissed Junior briefly on the lips. She stood back so she could look him in the eye. "But quashing your beef with Susan shows me that you are a man who loves his family enough to hold on to the ones he's got left, and that's Carl and Jerome. And me and our girls, and Sister True, and, when you think about it, even Susan."

"Besides," she said. "If you drop the case, then you don't need to see that young-ass lawyer no more, and that will really prove she don't mean nothing to you." Junior looked embarrassed.

"Just let it go, Lewis," Donetta said. She took his hands in hers. "It ain't your job to get Susan, that's up to the law and up to God. But it is your job to stand by your brother."

❧ CHAPTER 27 ✣

Jerome was silent as Susan sat beside him on the edge of their bed and told him everything. She started out by saying how scared she had been during his illness. She told him how desperately she wanted to help save his campaign and sit next to him as the First Lady of the city, and how hard she'd worked for his praise and admiration. Then, she tried to explain how humiliating it had been to have him start turning her down when she wanted to make love.

"It's one thing if the spirit is willing but the flesh is weak," she said. "After all, the doctors said to expect some changes in our love life. But it seemed like you didn't want to want me, and you didn't seem to care what it was doing to me either.

"I was working so hard and everyone was saying I was so smart and beautiful," she went on. "And I couldn't figure out why everyone but you could see it. So, I thought, well, if my husband doesn't want me, then I'll find someone who does."

"And that someone just happened to be Chancelly Foster's nephew?" Jerome couldn't believe it.

"The timing was just a coincidence," she said. "I never imagined in all my life I would ever run into that family again."

"I'm sure it brought up a lot of old stuff for you,"

Jerome said. Despite the shock, his voice was tender. As she looked at him, Susan realized it was the first time in all these years that she and her husband had talked about Chance.

"It did, but that doesn't matter," she said. "It just made things worse, and, in the end, I couldn't go through with it. It's like I suddenly came to my senses and realized that I was about to destroy my life with you. I got out of there as fast as I could, and I'm here telling you all of this now."

"So, Susan, let me get this straight." Jerome looked at his beautiful wife of so many long years. "You were about to let another man make love to you."

"I guess I just really needed to feel desirable again," Susan responded. She shook her head with shame. "Thank God I stopped before things went too far. Jerome, can you ever forgive me?"

"Susan, how could you ever think I didn't want you?" Jerome was incredulous. "After all these years, don't you know me better than that?"

"I do know you, Jerome, but you haven't been yourself lately."

"That's because I've been sick," he responded. "Like you said, the doctors told us what to expect: a temporary setback. My God, Susan, did you forget everything they said?"

"I know what they said, but it just wasn't as easy as all that, Jerome." Susan said. She shrugged helplessly. "I guess I thought I could prove those damn doctors wrong. A woman likes to think her man can't resist her and that her love can overcome anything."

"Even bone marrow replacement therapy?" Jerome raised his eyebrows.

"It really hurt my pride when I couldn't get you to respond to me," Susan admitted. She looked down at her hands. "So, I just had to get a response from someone else."

"This is unbelievable," Jerome said. He was still shaking his head in disbelief. "I think I need to take some time to think about this, Susan."

"You can take all the time you want, but you're my husband and I need your help, Jerome," Susan said. Though telling Jerome about her involvement with Craig had been agonizing, she had not lost her focus. Susan told Jerome that she needed money, how much she needed, and just where she expected him to get it from. "It's time we sold Hattie's house."

"I'm sorry, Susan. You know I love you, and I would do anything to help you, even now, but Ma'Dear's house and property are off the table. I hope my brothers will agree to sell it and go into business me."

"Really, Jerome?" Susan couldn't believe her ears. "Are you saying you won't help me with this now?"

"I want to help you, but I can't commit that money," Jerome said. "It's not just mine to give. Ma'Dear's property belongs to Carl and Junior too. Do you want me to ask if it would be okay with them?"

"Good heavens, no," Susan said hastily. She didn't want to imagine the explosion that would take place with the already-volatile brothers if they did that.

"But when you really think about it, they owe it us." She looked into her husband's amber eyes. "Neither one of them threw in a dime to help with Mother Durham's medical expenses. You and I nearly went broke."

"The timing was just bad for both of them," Jerome defended his brothers. "Junior just took a huge pay cut moving to a new agency, and Carl was up to his neck financing Deke's stake in the garage. You and I were better able to afford her care at the time."

"Well, still," Susan began. "We've got to do something."

For a moment, she and Jerome just stared at each other. He struggled to school his emotions. He couldn't believe some guy had the nerve to try to seduce his wife, and, even worse, she had been willing to go along with it. Despite being the most beautiful woman he had ever seen, his Susan remained high maintenance and insecure. She needed to be constantly reminded of her desirability, and, in his illness, he had failed her there. Still, that was no excuse for her disloyalty. Jerome found himself torn in his anger and confused by the situation.

"We will do something, Susan," he said. "Haven't I always protected you? I even let my poor mother put her life on the line for you, and we weren't even married yet. I just can't believe you were ready to throw this marriage away on a fling with another man."

His voice was bitter. He started to turn away, but Susan refused to let her guilt distract them from the matter at hand. She put her hand on his shoulder and turned him around to face her.

"Jerome, I know you have made sacrifices for me," she said. "And I have made sacrifices for you too. I've taken great risks. That's because we love each other so much. That hasn't changed."

"Exactly what sacrifices? What risks?" Jerome's golden eyes flamed. Susan took a step back, trembling, but then she held her chin up.

"You wouldn't be where you are today if it hadn't been for me," she said. "You would never have won that election. I made sure the public always saw you in your best light, and I kept your mother from ruining it for you."

Now, it was Jerome's turn to tremble. They had not spoken much about Hattie since her death, but, now, her ghost stood between them. Jerome knew his wife had worked hard to keep his mother quiet about what had really happened to Chancelly Foster so many years ago. But who had she really been protecting – him or herself? It was all one and the same. Any questions that could possibly come up about the young man's death so many years after the fact would still point to his guilt in the matter. He wasn't the one who had killed Chancelly. But he had helped cover it up, and he had lied about it all these years. Because of that, he had allowed Susan to control his mother during her illness, and, ultimately, he had allowed Susan to silence her.

He had never really admitted it to himself, but, looking at her now, he realized he had always known it to be true. Junior was right: Ma'Dear wouldn't have died the way she did if she hadn't been left alone with his treacherous Susan. She might even still be alive today, but he had been more interested in his career, had looked the other way, and let Susan "handle" things.

Jerome put his face in his hands. His wife watched him carefully. "All right," he said slowly. "First, we need to see if we can secure enough cash to deal with this. I'm not saying we should pay this guy off, but we need to make sure we have that option." Susan nodded, glad to see that Jerome was coming to his senses.

"I need to talk to Junior," he said. "I think he's still planning to come after you, and we need to turn that around and get him on our side in this thing."

"I think I might know a way," Susan said. She thought quickly about whether she should tell Jerome about seeing Junior with another woman, but then thought better of it. She would handle Junior herself, just as she had handled Hattie and anyone else who got in her way.

Susan started to say something else, but her voice trailed off as she focused on the TV.

"What is it?" Jerome turned to look.

The news was on. A blond anchor was presumably talking about a man and woman, whose pictures appeared in the corner of the screen. Susan quickly grabbed the remote and turned the volume up.

"... Foster-Lancet and her son, Dr. Craig Lancet, were found dead this evening of gunshot wounds in Mrs. Foster-Lancet's home in Barren Green Hills," the anchor stated. "An argument over a money matter is suspected to be the reason for what appears to be a murder-suicide. Lancet was holding a pistol when the mother and son were discovered by the victim's husband, James Lancet."

Jerome looked at his wife. The blood had drained from her face, leaving her as pale as marble as she stood there in shock. Susan collapsed.

CHAPTER 28

~ 6 months later ~

The Durham family and many of their friends were gathered with other members of the community at the official dedication ceremony of the Durham-Peace Community Center. Jerome, Carl, and Lewis, Jr., had decided to put the center on the site of their mother's old house. Part of the original structure would be preserved, forming the entrance of the impressive building which would now be the home of classes, activities and other services for families in their small but growing town of Sharon, Alabama. Though the brothers were heading up the project, the entire family was involved, and all were excited about the ceremony.

Susan Durham circulated among the growing crowd, smiling and shaking people's hands. Her campaigning efforts were proving to be successful. Her style and delivery were a lot more conservative than Jerome's had been, but people responded positively to her serious, intelligent handling of the issues, and she seemed to be headed for a win. Susan wore little makeup that day, and had her hair straight down and pulled back from her face with a simple headband. The style made her look young and vulnerable, Jerome thought, as he caught her eye across the room. Susan smiled faintly and calmly held his gaze, although her heart was racing like a teenaged girl's. She knew her husband, and playing it cool was the best way to get him hot. She turned out to be right. Jerome stood up and swiftly strolled to her side, stopping courteously but impatiently along the way to talk to the different people who approached him. Donetta and Trudy watched as Jerome whispered something to Susan. She nodded and smiled at him. As soon as he walked away, they went up to her.

The couple's separation had caught everyone by surprise, though both Jerome and Susan always described it as temporary. Donetta casually asked Susan how things were going with her estranged husband.

"It's going pretty well, I think," Susan responded, without hesitation. "He asked me to go out for ice cream after the celebration."

She felt pretty sure of herself. Jerome had every right to be angry with her, yet all he had asked for was a little time to get over his feelings. He had only packed a few things and never mentioned the word divorce at all. Susan felt the security that had been a part of her life ever since she had married the man start to trickle back, even though he was still sleeping at a hotel. Jerome still loved her. He knew everything that she had done and still called her every day.

To Susan's surprise, the separation had not been as tough as she thought it would be. She threw herself into her work and, not surprisingly, the intense focus paid off. She was doing even better in the polls than she had expected.

Her sisters-in-law had been so supportive during the last few months. Donetta had been steadfast the whole time. Trudy had taken a little longer to come around, but she had proven dependable as well, and she always had encouraging words for Susan. "Jerome will be back," she said. "I don't think he could live without you. He's never loved anyone else."

"Thank you, True," Susan said. Real sincerity was in her voice, and she felt that Trudy was right. Though Jerome had felt the separation was necessary, he had been appalled at the idea that Susan had felt he had neglected her, and he promised things would be different. Jerome wanted to make his wife feel like the only woman in the world, and, so far, he was doing a great job of it. It was just a matter of time before he moved back home. In the meantime, Susan was enjoying being courted by her handsome husband again. He had never stopped loving her, and it would only be a matter of time before he moved back into their home to be with her. She and Jerome had turned out to have the kind of ride-or-die love that these young kids were always talking about in their music videos and such.

"And how is Carl doing?" Susan asked politely. Though she talked with Jerome every day, she hadn't had much contact with his brothers.

"He's coming along," Trudy said. The subject of Carl's mental state was still touchy. "Of course, some days are better than others, but I think he's making some good progress. Pastor Solomon has been working a lot with him. But I really think it's working on this project with his brothers that's doing him some real good."

"It's been good for all of them," Donetta agreed. "Susan, I think you should talk to Junior."

She smiled at the three brothers, who were talking to a growing crowd of people. One of them in particular caught Susan's eye – a tall, impeccably dressed woman with a professional air. It was the woman Susan had seen Junior with at the hotel. Who exactly was she, and what was she doing there?

Susan knew she had literally dodged a bullet with the deaths of Craig Lancet and Eleanor Foster-Lancet. The scandal with those two was no longer a threat to her campaign, but Lewis, Jr., still was. If he was having an affair with that woman, there had to be a way to use it against him to keep him quiet.

"Donetta," Susan said casually. "Who is that?" She gestured with her chin toward Beverly Epperson.

"Oh, that's Junior's lawyer," Donetta said just as casually. She saw the look of shock on her sister-in-law's face. Susan was reeling. If that woman was a lawyer, did that mean Lewis really planned to pursue his accusations against her in his mother's death? Had they followed her to the hotel that night? What did they know? Susan tried to control her panic. Donetta patted her arm soothingly.

"You don't need to worry about her, Susan," Donetta said. "I talked to Junior. He's not going to try to reopen Mother Durham's case. He's just thankful that his brothers are talking again."

Susan was visibly relieved. "Thank you, Donetta." Jerome moving out had been bad enough. Being implicated in a death investigation would have been a disaster. "The campaign ..."

"I know, honey," Donetta soothed. She had seamlessly transitioned from Jerome's campaign to Susan's and had even helped conceal their separation from the media. Susan had grown entirely dependent on her, and she knew it. "It's going to be all right, but you need to talk to Junior. Sometimes a man just needs to hear the truth."

Donetta caught Junior's eye and nodded, then walked away, leaving Susan there with her thoughts. Susan was still trying to compose herself when Junior came up and stood beside her, as if on cue. For a moment they stood in silence, watching as RJ and Albertina Peace arrived and Jerome walked up to greet them.

RJ had given into gentle pressure from Albertina, as well as his own curiosity, and agreed to meet Jerome. Over the past several weeks, the two men, along with Carl and Lewis, Jr., had been getting to know one another.

"Susie," Junior said. Susan controlled her reaction to the nickname. He knew she was just doing it to belittle her. "Did you hear what my wife said?"

"About a man needing to hear the truth, right?" Susan responded, without looking up.

"Yes," Junior replied. He, too, stared straight ahead. Jerome was leading RJ and Albertina around, proudly introducing them to people.

"Yes, I heard what she said," Susan said. She finally looked at him. "But first, just let me thank you for putting an end to this craziness over Mother Durham's death. There's a lot at stake and it probably would have hurt more people than it would have helped."

"I agree."

Susan looked straight ahead again. "All right, so, the truth." For a moment she stood silently, searching for the right words. Finally, she spoke again.

"Lewis, your mother once asked me if I had ever done anything bad for love." She looked at him again. "I couldn't even answer the question until she died, and, by then, the answer was 'yes.'"

She held his gaze, allowing her words to sink in. Junior's face remained impassive, but she thought she saw a little tremor in his facial muscles, a painful shift in his eyes. He was digesting the truth that he had known along and that she had finally admitted to. But Junior shocked Susan with his next words.

"I know the only reason my mother ever put up with you is because she knew you would take care of Jerome," he said. "She knew you would do whatever it took to protect him, even if she was the one you had to protect him from."

Fighting back tears, Susan nodded silently. Junior met her eyes again for a silent moment, then nodded and walked away. Susan pushed her hands back through her hair, sighing with relief. It was over. She could get on with her life. She could still win her campaign. Could she win back Jerome, too? At least now she would be free to try.

After a moment, she rejoined Donetta and Trudy where the rest of the family stood for the unveiling of the art that graced the front hall of the community center. Junior pulled Donetta into his arms and their twin daughters crowded into the hug. Carl, Trudy, RJ, Frankie and Albertina smiled as Jerome held out his hand to Susan.

The painting Jerome had commissioned by a local artist for the occasion depicted a group of young people gathered in a playground. Jerome had requested that the artist portray different members of the family in an inspirational setting. The artist had done brilliantly, using a combination of photographs, in-person meetings, imagination, and skill. The result was a beautiful work of art.

A young girl with long brown braids might have been Susan at age 12 or so. She was watching another three girls at jump rope. The girl dancing in the ropes had sparkling eyes and a set of dimples that could only be Donetta. A tall, smiling teen dangling from a basketball hoop looked a lot like Lewis, Jr.

Trudy had told the artist how she and Carl had met, when Trudy had been hired to tutor him in high school math. Their story had inspired the artist to paint a young couple reading a book on a bench. Elsewhere in the painting, two amber-eyed boys, alike enough to be twins, played a game of marbles on a nearby sidewalk. The skillful artist had painted the two of them after meeting RJ and Jerome.

At the center of the painting, a young woman with a full-lipped smile was watching over children playing in a fountain. Barefoot in the water, in a bright blue dress and a straw hat full of flowers, the Hattie Durham in the painting was still innocent and girlish. Her gleaming eyes and hopeful figure truly symbolized the meaning of the Durham-Peace Community Center. That name had two meanings to her sons, who had accepted a new brother into the family and had ended a war among themselves.

The painting was colorful and optimistic. And

inscribed on a gold plate on the frame beneath its frame was its title: *Every Child Deserves to Be Loved.*

In the picture, a young, beautiful Hattie Durham smiled.

THE END